'Panicking at the thought of a kiss, Rosalind?' Kurt's husky voice was mocking.

'Not in the least,' she lied. 'It doesn't throw me into a panic because the fire went out of our relationship two years ago. You can't breathe life back into cold ashes. Now, goodnight.'

Her parting line delivered, she took a step towards the stairs and then gave a little gasp as Kurt caught hold of her.

Far from resisting, she found herself meeting his kiss exactly as if she had been expecting it. Everything, from their low-key sparring to his sarcasm and her flashes of temper, had served to make it the inevitable conclusion to the warm sultry night.

'It seems you were wrong,' Kurt said quietly. 'The ashes of our relationship aren't cold and lifeless, not by a long shot.'

Books you will enjoy
by JENNY ARDEN

ARROGANT INVADER

There had never been much love lost between Gwenyth and Jeb Hunter, though now he seemed determined to pursue her. But Gwenyth was happily engaged to Marc and planning a future in France, so what was there for her to be afraid of?

FRAGILE PARADISE

Genieve certainly hadn't meant to get involved with Ross Macauley, not after the way she had been hurt so recently. Anyway, didn't Ross belong to Coralie, Genieve's cousin? Ross didn't seem to think so—and it appeared that what he intended was to sweep Genieve off her feet...

AN UNFINISHED AFFAIR

BY
JENNY ARDEN

MILLS & BOON LIMITED
ETON HOUSE 18-24 PARADISE ROAD
RICHMOND SURREY TW9 1SR

All the characters in this book have no existence outside the imagination of the Author, and have no relation whatsoever to anyone bearing the same name or names. They are not even distantly inspired by any individual known or unknown to the Author, and all the incidents are pure invention.

All Rights Reserved. The text of this publication or any part thereof may not be reproduced or transmitted in any form or by any means, electronic or mechanical, including photocopying, recording, storage in an information retrieval system, or otherwise, without the written permission of the publisher.

This book is sold subject to the condition that it shall not, by way of trade or otherwise, be lent, resold, hired out or otherwise circulated without the prior consent of the publisher in any form of binding or cover other than that in which it is published and without a similar condition including this condition being imposed on the subsequent purchaser.

First published in Great Britain 1991 by Mills & Boon Limited

© Jenny Arden 1991

Australian copyright 1991 Philippine copyright 1991 This edition 1991

ISBN 0 263 77187 3

Set in Times Roman 11 on 11½ pt. 01-9108-48868 C

Made and printed in Great Britain

CHAPTER ONE

THE gardens of the Quinta Buganvilea, which belonged to the Summervilles, one of the prominent English families in Madeira, were some of the most beautiful on the island. Beyond the well-manicured lawns were terraced borders that were ablaze with roses, hibiscus and strelitzia.

The french windows of the white-colonnaded *quinta* were ajar and a woman in her early twenties pushed them open. She was strikingly pretty, with chestnut hair cut in a burnished bob that just brushed her shoulders. She had a warm, glowing complexion, high cheekbones and a pointed chin. Her mouth was sensitive, but firm.

Though all her features were pleasing, ironically it was her eyes that held the key to her allure. Fringed with long dark lashes, they were brown with flecks of gold radiating out from the pupils, and as fascinating as the flame of a candle.

In a sleeveless blouse and crisp white trousers she was slim and graceful, at one with the serene and idyllic setting. Yet her mood was totally at variance with it as she paused on the threshold. Immediately she was aware of the different quality to the light, not because she could see it, but because the sun felt warm on her face and arms.

Counting the steps she took, she crossed the veranda. Six steps and she stopped. Her questing hand grazed the smooth curved back of one of the bamboo armchairs. She sat down in it and bit her lip. Her fingers were clenched tightly into her palms.

Normally at eleven-thirty she would have been hard at work indoors in her studio, completely absorbed. But today her thoughts were in chaos and, rather than ruin the figure she was modelling in clay, she had decided to abandon it for the time being.

'Damn, damn, damn!' she cried suddenly, using anger to ease the feelings of rawness and vulnerability inside her.

She had some reason to be put out with her aunt, but most of all she was angry with Kurt Wilding, wildly and blazingly angry. She had wanted to forget him, to keep the door firmly shut on her broken romance. When she had left London and returned to Madeira she hadn't expected their paths ever to cross again. Instead, thanks to Julia, she was about to be forced into his company, and she would have done almost anything to avoid it.

She didn't want to be reminded of how much she had once loved him, or of the callous way he had treated her. To remember was to have all the pain, bitterness and hurt come surging to the surface again.

She swallowed hard, trying to master her emotions, but it was no use. There was a tight ache beneath her ribs and she wanted very much to cry. She had believed she had got over the heartbreak of her love-affair. Now she realised bitterly that it had been a delusion. She had no more forgotten Kurt's cruel rejection of her than, deep down, despite her courageous pretence, she had accepted the loss of her sight.

As if sensing her distress, the chocolate-point Siamese that had been basking in a sunny spot on the veranda came and jumped up on her lap. The cat, which her father had given her, wore a red collar with a little bell. That way, although Cleo moved on such silent velvet paws, Rosalind could always hear where the cat was and there was no danger of her being tripped up.

Cleo settled down on her lap and began to purr contentedly. But although the little cat appeared to doze, she was quick to detect that someone had come into the garden. Her head lifted a split second before Rosalind, too, heard footsteps. A few moments later a well-dressed man rounded the corner of the house and came up the steps on to the veranda.

'Hello, Rosalind.'

The ache beneath her ribs was as cruel as ever, but, recognising the baritone voice, she smiled a welcome. Manuel Pereiros was a partner in the wine-shipping business owned by her father and a close family friend.

In his late thirties, he had closely trimmed dark hair that showed some grey at the temples. Laughter lines were etched at the corners of his eyes. His jaw was strong.

'Manuel, what a nice surprise!' she began. 'What brings you here this morning?'

'You, of course,' he quipped. 'I've been visiting some of the vineyards and, as I was passing, I thought I'd drop in before going on to the office.' He sat down alongside her on one of the cane armchairs. As his gaze swept over the gardens he observed, 'It's always so wonderfully quiet and peaceful here.'

'It's very quiet at the moment with Dad away on business. And Julia's gone to the airport this morning,' Rosalind explained.

She spoke calmly, though inwardly she was anything but calm. She felt angry and trapped. In an hour at most Kurt would be arriving at the *quinta*. Her heart began to thud unevenly, a strange reaction to a man she would always hate. Kurt had made her love him and then he had tossed her aside.

Was it really only two years ago that she had first met him? It seemed a lifetime ago, while she seemed almost a different person, she had changed so much.

She still had the same redhead's temper, she supposed, though these days it remained well hidden. There had been so many difficulties to overcome connected with going blind that she'd learned not to explode over trivia. Her disability, too, seemed to have robbed her of her confidence, her exuberance. She was no longer the impulsive girl who had caught the attention of Kurt Wilding and nor, thanks to him, was she the naïve romantic she had been once.

'Why is Julia driving to the airport?' Manuel's enquiry broke into her thoughts. 'I understood your father wasn't coming back from New York till next week.'

'He's not,' she confirmed, and then explained, 'The architect Julia's engaged is arriving from London today. She's gone to meet him.'

Julia had lived in Lisbon for the last ten years. Following her divorce, Rosalind's father had persuaded his sister to come back home and make a fresh start. He'd reminded her that she owned a plot of land outside Camacha which would make a lovely site for a house, but had said that she was more than welcome to stay at the *quinta* for as long as she liked.

'I'm surprised Julia wants a house of her own,' Manuel remarked. 'There's so much room here.'

'More than enough,' Rosalind agreed. 'But, as you know, it looks as if Dad will marry again and I've an idea that has something to do with her decision. It's not that she and Isobel don't get along, but I think she feels she'd be a bit *de trop* if she stayed.'

'And how will you feel if your father remarries?' Manuel asked, his astute eyes on her face which looked strangely wan this morning.

'I'm glad Dad's found someone who makes him happy,' she answered, trying hard not to be selfish.

She knew her father had been lonely over the years, for all he had hidden it so well. Rosalind had been seven when her mother had died. It was generally assumed that with a young daughter to bring up Bernard Summerville would remarry after a time. Certainly he'd had plenty of opportunity. He was successful and charming and through his business enterprises he had many social contacts. Instead he'd chosen to remain a widower.

Before she'd lost her sight Rosalind would have been delighted that her father had found someone that he wished to marry. Now things were different. It wasn't that she had anything against Isobel. She didn't, but she knew her father wouldn't hear of her getting a small place of her own, and she had reservations about sharing her home with a stepmother.

'So it's not that,' Manuel said cryptically.

'It's not what?' Rosalind asked in puzzlement.

'You're upset about something.'

'Nonsense! I'm fine. Honestly I am.' Her protesting laugh echoed mockingly in her ears. Changing the topic, she said, 'I'm sure it's time for coffee. Can I offer you a cup?'

'Thanks, that would be nice.'

'I'll ask Maria to bring it out on to the veranda.'

'No, I'll go,' Manuel insisted. 'You stay where you are.'

When he returned she was sitting exactly as she had been when he had left her, with the Siamese asleep on her lap. 'I wonder if Cleo knows she was the model for your last brilliant set of sculptures,' Manuel remarked as he sat down.

'Cleo doesn't bother about things like that,' Rosalind said, summoning up a smile. 'As long as she can bask in the sun, or chase butterflies across the lawn, she's happy.'

'While you, unless I'm very much mistaken, are not.'

'What makes you jump to that conclusion?' she demanded, tucking a silken strand of hair behind her ear.

'You, my dear,' Manuel said, 'are putting on a very brave act, though why I don't know. Do you think I didn't sense something was wrong the moment I came on to the veranda and found you sitting here?'

'I can't be at work in my studio all the time!' she protested jokingly.

She received no reply. Manuel evidently didn't buy her answer.

'Oh, all right,' she capitulated, realising that a pretence was useless with Manuel. He knew her too well. 'It's Julia.'

'Julia? What's she done?'

'Nothing, really. I'm being stupid. When she said she was going to build a house I assumed she'd hire a local architect. I'd no idea until she told me so last night that she'd engaged Kurt Wilding to draw up the plans for it.'

Manuel's dark brows came together, his frown mirrored in his impatient tone. 'Good heavens! How could she be so insensitive!'

'Perhaps she thought I wouldn't mind.' She was tightly in command of herself. 'After all, it's getting on for two years since Kurt and I were engaged. And he'll only be staying for a week. It's bound to be a little awkward, but I expect I'll survive.'

They were interrupted by Maria, who brought the coffee out on to the veranda. Rosalind could tell from the aroma that it was Manuel's favourite blend. The silver coffee spoons tinkled daintily against the fine porcelain.

She located the handle of the coffee-pot, only to have Manuel say. 'It's OK. I'll pour. How do you feel about meeting Kurt again?' There was a probing note in the casually framed question.

The truth was, she didn't think she could bear it. She accepted the cup Manuel handed to her, appalled at how nearly she had said so out loud. Careful to keep her voice steady, she dodged the question.

'I can't understand why Julia didn't tell me she'd asked him to draw up the plans for the house.'

'Perhaps she didn't mention it because she didn't want to upset you,' Manuel suggested.

'In which case why did she invite him here?' There was more emotion in her voice than she would have wished. She made an effort to continue in a more even tone, 'I know Kurt's in a class of his own as an architect, but there are others quite capable of designing the sort of house Julia wants.'

'You're suspicious she might be matchmaking?' Manuel questioned.

As it happened, that thought hadn't crossed Rosalind's mind.

'For all I know Kurt could be engaged, or even married,' she said. Tonelessly she went on, 'He was very keen to have a son.'

Manuel's gaze narrowed perceptively on her face. Her unseeing eyes were dark and lustrous. The sunshine picked out the coppery lights in her chestnut hair. One hand continued to caress the gently purring Siamese on her knee.

'Sometimes I wonder if deep down you really are as cool and contained as you appear,' he remarked reflectively.

'What makes you say that?' she asked.

'Simply this,' he answered. 'When I look at your art I see a passion in it. No matter what you take as a subject, your sculptures are always realistic, bold. I'm not an art critic, but, in my opinion, the fisherman mending his nets, commissioned by the Lisbon Gallery, is one of the finest sculptures you've ever done. It tells me that your work, apart from being a vehicle for your enormous talent, is like a safety valve. And that, in a way, is sad, while at the same time I ask myself how much longer you can sublimate your feelings through your art.'

'Forever is the answer to that. When I'm at work in my studio I forget everything.'

But the truth was, his words struck a chill. Kurt hadn't even arrived yet and already she was in turmoil, unable to proceed with the figure she was currently modelling. Always till now she'd been able to lose herself in her art. Supposing the charm were to fail her? It was a worrying thought.

There was a short pause. She sensed Manuel's discerning gaze on her.

'You never would tell me the cause of your broken engagement,' he said speculatively, 'but it's my belief you're still in love with Kurt Wilding.'

She laughed at the idea. After the way Kurt had rejected her she'd have to be a masochist to be in love with him still. She would never forgive him for all the pain he had caused her.

'Finding out that Julia's invited him here was a shock, that's all,' she said. The past hurt too much for her to want to talk about it, even with so good a friend as Manuel. She continued, 'I admit I'd avoid seeing him if I could, but short of stowing away on one of the ships in the harbour—not a very practical idea—there doesn't seem any way I can escape from here at such short notice.'

Her determined effort to make light of Kurt's visit so that Manuel would stop questioning her paid off. She heard the smile in his voice as he answered, 'I'd offer you safe refuge at my place, only I'm afraid that's not a very practical suggestion either'.

'It isn't,' she agreed with a laugh. 'Can you imagine the gossip it would cause if I were to move in with you?'

'Only too well, unfortunately. You wouldn't have a reputation left. So, since giving you sanctuary is out of the question let me take you out to dinner instead.'

'It's kind of you to ask me——'

'I'm not being kind,' he insisted, cutting across her. 'I enjoy your company and I'd ask you out more often if it weren't so difficult to prise you away from the *quinta*.'

'It's just that I feel more relaxed on home ground,' she explained. 'I have a clear mental picture of the house and the garden and I can move about pretty well. I don't have to worry about bumping into things or being clumsy.'

'I understand how you feel, but, just the same, I'm not going to take no for an answer.'

'Are you bullying me?' she teased.

'A little,' he said with humour. 'It's good for you. Now, is it settled that we're having dinner together?'

'Yes, it's settled,' she smiled, conscious of a sense of relief that for one evening at least she wouldn't have to steel herself to make polite conversation with Kurt when what she felt like even after all this time was demanding how he could have been so hard.

'Is seven o'clock too early for me to pick you up?' Manuel asked.

'Seven will be fine.'

'Good,' he answered. The cane chair creaked as he got to his feet. 'And now I must be going or it will be lunchtime before I get to the office. *Até a vista*. I'll see you later, my dear.'

He patted her arm in farewell. She heard his steps grow fainter and then listened as the birds came to life in the morning quietness. She could hear them fluttering and calling to one another in a nearby tree.

Surrounded by its high white wall, the *quinta* and its quiet grounds had until now been private and unassailable, a haven where Rosalind had started to rebuild her life after the double blow of losing her sight and breaking up with Kurt. She checked her braille watch. Julia had left for the airport at Santa Cruz just after eleven, which meant that in no time at all her tranquil haven would be shattered.

Tipping the sleepy cat off her lap, she stood up and went indoors. Her current sculpture was fraught with difficulties and she was still in no mood to give it her full attention, but neither was she inclined to spend the whole morning in a storm of turmoil.

She turned the doorknob and went into her studio. North-facing, it was bright but cool. She pulled on her smock and then crossed over to the main workbench. Several large storage bins stood beneath it and from one of them she took out as much red earthenware clay as she could hold.

The clay, which was delivered to the *quinta* by her suppliers, was described as 'prepared', but it needed to be wedged thoroughly before it was used to make it consistent in colour and texture. She banged the heavy lump down on the bench and began to pummel it into shape. The rougher the treatment it received, the better.

Wedging was hard work and she paused to brush back a stray stand of hair from her face before continuing, swinging her arms with an easy rhythm. She halved the earthenware oblong in front of her a second time and threw the cut off wedge firmly against the slab which lay on the bench. The aggressive handling of the clay did her good, making her feel stronger.

She couldn't avoid meeting Kurt again, but she could be cold, polite and distant with him. There was no way she was going to let him see how devastated she had been by her discovery of how little she meant to him.

She tensed, hearing the sound of a car drawing up outside the *quinta*. With her ex-fiancé under the same roof as her, there was no possibility of her concentrating even on the mechanical task of wedging clay. Covering it with a damp cloth to stop it drying out, she went over to the sink to wash her hands.

Slowly she unbuttoned her smock and took it off. She couldn't check her intense pent-up anger with Kurt for coming here. Having caused her so much pain, he had no right to walk boldly back into her life. It was a measure of his heartless insensitivity that he dared to.

Resentment against him stiffening her spirit, she left her studio and went into the hall. She entered the drawing-room, and then suddenly stopped. A prickling stirred at the back of her neck. Despite the stillness in the room, her senses were so finely attuned that she knew without a doubt that someone was standing by the french windows.

Her heart began to thump unevenly as she caught the faint spicy fragrance of a man's aftershave. She had wanted to greet Kurt coldly and casually. Instead, conscious in every nerve of his masculine presence, she found that her mouth was dry and that, like a fawn at bay, it was all she could do to stand her ground, such was the awareness filling the room.

She didn't need her lost sight to be able to visualise his rugged face, the gleaming dark hair that fell over his forehead, the patrician features, forcefully carved. The sunlight was bright in the room and his eyes, hard as chips of flint, would be slightly narrowed on her in appraisal.

Though it was no more than a few seconds it seemed to her a fraught eternity before he spoke.

'Hello, Rosalind.'

His slightly husky resolute voice was achingly familiar. She had always been shatteringly conscious of his tall, powerful frame and virile maleness. That consciousness remained, even though she was now blind and no longer loved him. Not only was his voice that of a man used to giving orders and having others obey, but it fell on her ears as she would have expected from someone of his height.

She went towards the sofa. Her legs felt shaky and she was glad to sit down before asking distantly, 'Hello, Kurt. Did you have a good journey?'

Footsteps brought him closer.

'Hardly the most original greeting after two years,' he commented with mockery.

Her chin tilted a fraction, but her voice was very calm as she answered, 'I'm not a very original person.'

'I don't agree. Original, wilful and unpredictable is how I'd describe you.'

'Is that meant to be a compliment?' she asked.

'Do you want me to compliment you?'

'No, not particularly,' she answered carelessly in response to the sardonic question.

She threaded her fingers tightly together as Kurt sat down opposite her. She heard the cushions rustle as he leant back, her imagination providing her with a perfect picture of him.

A sensation of being closely scrutinised by piercing blue eyes tingled through her. She was intensely aware of his nearness, memories and the bitterness they evoked meaning that it was impossible for her even to attempt to be calmly aloof with him as she had intended.

Moistening her lips, she asked, 'Where's Julia?'

'Why, are you afraid of being alone with me?' She had the impression of a dark eyebrow raised mockingly in her direction.

'Not in the least,' she denied. 'If you came here thinking I'd be disturbed by your arrival you're going to be sadly disappointed.'

'What makes you imagine I thought of you at all?'

The offhand yet cutting question was like a slap in the face. She paled a little but, refusing to let him see that even now he had the power to hurt her, she gave a droll, slightly dry reply.

'Feminine conceit, obviously.'

Kurt's laugh was spontaneous, if slightly shaded with contempt. Amusement making his voice rather less abrasive, he said, 'You haven't changed. You always were quick when it came to repartee.'

'I don't expect you've changed much either,' she said, thinking of the past.

'I wouldn't say that,' he answered. 'I'm a little more cynical than I used to be.'

'Is that remark aimed at me by any chance?' she asked, certain that it was and stung, though she didn't show it, by his blatant hypocrisy.

'What makes you think that?' he answered sardonically.

'If anyone has the right to be cynical I think it's me!'

'I have to admit, I was surprised when Julia told me you're still single,' he drawled. To her his reply seemed a complete *non sequitur*. 'I was sure you'd be married by now. What happened to the inestimable Andrew?'

'I can't see that's any affair of yours,' she returned.

'We were engaged once. I wouldn't be human not still to be vaguely interested in you.'

She bit back the retort that from the start all he had ever been was vaguely interested in her, or rather interested in his own ends. Instead she answered calmly, 'I decided I like being single. It means I'm able to concentrate on my work.'

'Your aunt tells me you devote practically every minute to it.'

'Is there anything wrong with that?' she asked.

'Nothing at all.' His answer suggested a shrug. 'I understand you're making quite a name for yourself in the art world.'

'Luckily being blind isn't a handicap when it comes to sculpture,' she told him. Even, she thought wryly, if it was a handicap with regard to marriage. 'I've always enjoyed using clay as a medium. It's somehow exciting to take a shapeless lump of Raku or red earthenware, to model it into something beautiful and then to see it through the rigours of firing.'

'Just the same, it must have been very hard for you to know you'd never use oils and canvas again.'

'It was, but I produce better results with clay than I ever did with an easel,' she answered. She didn't need his compassion, if that was what had prompted his remark. She was too stubborn and too proud.

'What do the specialists say about your sight? I take it you've had the best,' he said.

'I don't want your hypocritical concern!'

'For God's sake!' he exclaimed, his voice clipped he went on, 'I merely wondered what sort of treatment you'd had.'

'There's nothing more that can be done,' she told him. Striving to keep control of her emotions, she continued, 'In a very few cases the condition I'm suffering from improves, but for most people the blindness is permanent. But I think we've talked enough about me. How about you? Are you married now?'

'Speculating on whether there's a chance of us rekindling our affair?'

His mockery made her fingers itch to slap him. He had meant everything to her, and his gibe was almost more than she could endure. But, refusing to rise to his sarcasm, she answered calmly, 'No, I was just curious. As you said earlier, one never quite loses interest in an old love.'

'So I did,' he murmured. It was evident from his tone that her neat turning of his earlier remark to her advantage amused him, albeit in a dry sort of way. 'Well, since you're interested, no, I'm not married.'

'Vivienne must be pleased.' She made the sweetly barbed statement in spite of herself.

'And what exactly am I supposed to deduce from that remark?' he asked.

His voice, ominously quiet, set her heart thumping. Conscious of a sense of redress, because she had succeeded in touching him on the raw, she answered, 'Vivienne might not have been prepared to divorce her husband for you, but she certainly didn't want to let go of you.'

'Jealous, Rosalind?' he taunted softly.

'It seems I'm not the only one who's conceited! Just as you haven't spared me a thought these last two years, I haven't spared you one either.'

Kurt laughed at her cool reply, and Julia, who came in at that moment, observed, evidently totally unaware of the sparks of confrontation that charged the atmosphere, 'It sounds as if the two of you are getting on like a house on fire.'

'We've been doing some catching up,' Kurt drawled. 'We must pick up on this conversation again some time, Rosalind.'

On the surface it sounded nothing more than a genial remark from an old flame, but, with her hearing sharpened by the loss of her sight, and aware of his satirical gaze on her, Rosalind knew otherwise. A defensive prickling ran over her skin. Kurt's words were a statement of intent, almost a warning, but if he expected her to take back one word she had said about his precious mistress he'd be waiting a very long time!

CHAPTER TWO

'Lunch is ready now, so shall we go outside?' Julia suggested.

Rosalind got to her feet, and then, as she realised Kurt was beside her, found that her heart was racing. As though guiding a blind person was the most natural thing in the world, he tucked her hand companionably through his arm. In view of the fact that he had walked out of her life because she was losing her sight, she didn't need him now to walk her out to the patio.

'I'm quite capable of finding my own way, thank you,' she said shortly, the unexpected physical contact a further assault on her already fragile emotions.

She made to free herself, but Kurt's firm hand closed over hers, forestalling her.

'Then you don't need to prove it to me, do you?' he returned.

'Have you any idea how arrogant and overbearing you can be? I've said I don't need your help,' she insisted.

'And have you any idea how arrogant and overbearing I'm going to be it you don't stop being so stubborn?'

There was a shading of humour in his voice but the threat was there none the less. With little option but to concede defeat, she allowed him to escort her to her place at the table on the patio. The discovery that part of her actually appreciated his gentle guidance infuriated her still more.

His forearm was strong and leanly muscled. She hoped he didn't notice that her hand, which rested on it, trembled slightly. Much as she despised him, physically she still responded to his masculine appeal.

The patio was a very pleasant place to have lunch. Decorative stone tubs, each overflowing with greenery and flowers, marked its perimeter and the fragrance of blossoms drifted on the air. Bougainvillaea tumbled in a mass of deep mauve stars over the nearby wall of the house.

The sunlight sparkled with diamond brilliance off the fountain that was playing, the tranquil sound echoed by quiet birdsongs. Dragon trees framed a dramatic view over the orchards and vineyards which swept down in a tapestry of every shade of green to the town of Funchal and the dazzlingly blue sea.

The timbre of Kurt's voice as he chatted to Julia over the first course told Rosalind that he was completely relaxed. In contrast she could do little more than play with her food, though she managed to contribute to the conversation with a composure that was no less convincing for being counterfeit. The epitome of calm, Manuel had called her. What frightened her was that her calm was that of a dormant volcano.

During dessert, a mouthwatering concoction of pineapple, strawberries and figs in brandy, Kurt said, 'I can see why Madeira is called "the island of flowers". The Garden of Eden couldn't have surpassed this for a setting.'

'It's because the island's such a paradise that it's so popular with honeymoon couples,' Julia replied. 'It's a perfect place for romantics.'

'It helps, too, that the weather's always so good,' Rosalind added her token comment.

'Surely love's above the vagaries of the weather?' Kurt's voice was mocking.

'Ideally,' she murmured, wondering what the consequences would be if she were to dash the contents of her wine glass in his swarthy face.

'If only love were always ideal,' Julia murmured with a sigh. The remark was prompted by her recent divorce. She quickly gave a little laugh, shrugging off her regrets. 'This is getting far too philosophical,' she joked. 'I was about to suggest that we go to Reid's tonight. It's a must for every visitor to Funchal. What do you say?'

The world-famous hotel was noted for its superb cuisine and sub-tropical gardens, and most tourists, even if they couldn't afford to stay there, at least splashed out with tea on the terrace at Reid's.

Rosalind began to answer her aunt at the same time that Kurt spoke. Immediately she broke off but he deferred to her with an ironically polite, 'I'm sorry. You were saying.'

Her mouth tightened a little. His satirical attitude was taxing her temper.

'Only that I'm afraid you'll have to count me out,' she said.

'I know you prefer eating at home, but make an exception for once,' Julia said, trying to persuade her.

'That's just it,' she answered. 'I have made an exception. Manuel's asked me to have dinner with him tonight.'

'When did you arrange that?' There was a note of surprise in Julia's voice.

'This morning.' Footsteps sounded on the patio as Rosalind explained, 'He stopped by on his way to the office.'

'Senhora Martin, there's a telephone call for you.' The housekeeper addressed her aunt.

'Thank you, Maria.' There was a slight scrape of a chair on the stone as Julia stood up. 'Will the two of you excuse me a moment?'

Left alone with Kurt, Rosalind searched a perfectly blank mind for something innocuous to say. If it had been taxing to make small talk with him while her aunt had been present, it was doubly hard now.

She sensed Kurt studying her, his head tilted in an attitude of appraisal, his blue eyes piercing and direct. Self-consciously she took a sip of coffee, her pulse quickening in the silence. She didn't love him any more but he still had the power to play havoc with her senses.

'Who's Manuel?' he asked finally. 'A friend?'

'Yes, a friend,' she said, setting her cup down on its saucer.

Though her father had never said as much, she had a hunch it would have pleased him to have Manuel as a son-in-law. There was no doubt he would have made her an excellent husband. He was considerate, conscientious and steady. More than that, and far more importantly as far as she was concerned, she believed that her blindness would have made no difference to him.

But though she liked him very much she wasn't in love with him and never had been. He knew it and then had settled for a warm, uncomplicated friendship. But she saw no need to explain all that to Kurt.

She didn't know quite where their conversation was heading but instinctively she was on her guard.

'That's rather a vague term,' Kurt commented, repeating it, 'a "friend".'

'You were the one who used it,' she pointed out.

'Well, maybe you'd like to expand on the cliché,' he drawled with a touch of sarcasm.

'What cliché?' She felt raw inside with the turbulent feelings meeting Kurt again had unleashed, but no provocation was going to make her flare up with him. He had never loved her and pride demanded that she let him think from her cool behaviour that she had put their broken engagement behind her as easily as he had.

'The "just good friends" cliché. Is Manuel your latest boyfriend?'

'Did you come here to interrogate me?' she asked.

'I'd hardly call it an interrogation.' He laughed drily. 'Or have you become such a recluse that you interpret any opening conversational gambit that way these days?'

'What makes you think I've become a recluse?' she asked.

'Not only do you spend all your time in your studio, but from what's just been said I gather it's difficult to persuade you to leave the *quinta* even for a meal out.'

'I happen to prefer eating at home,' she told him.

'You used to enjoy going out to dinner.'

'That was before...' she replied, and then broke off as she realised that she was beginning to snap. It hurt to be reminded of the romantic evenings they had shared, hurt because in reality there had been nothing romantic about them. Kurt had decided he wanted a wife and an heir and had set out to win her with calculated charm. She continued coolly, 'Being blind, it's only too easy to knock over a wine glass or to find my steak's disappeared from my fork en route to my mouth. I don't like making a spectacle of myself in public.'

'Aren't you being a little oversensitive?' he asked.

'Oh, that's good coming from you!'

'Would you care to explain that remark?' he asked, dangerously bland.

Her slim shoulders hunched in an eloquently negligent shrug.

'No, I wouldn't,' she said, taking another sip of coffee.

In the silence that followed her calmly defiant answer she was as aware, as if she could see it, of the tight set of Kurt's masculine mouth.

'If you dislike eating out,' he said, 'then why didn't you invite your boyfriend to have dinner here?'

'Manuel's not ...' she denied, and then decided to let his assumption stand. If nothing else it would establish that she was completely over their affair. Amending her reply, she said, 'Manuel talked me into it.'

'I hope I'm not driving you away.' Despite the mocking inflexion in Kurt's attractively husky voice, Rosalind sensed that eyes as keen and probing as a psychiatrist's were narrowed on her.

She pushed her cup further on to the table, determined that her answer would be far too composed for him to divine that he had hit on the truth. Shading her voice lightly with amusement, she said,

'Now you're being oversensitive. It's nothing to me that you're staying here.'

'Good, then one evening you and I must go out for a meal, perhaps talk over old times.'

She shook her head. 'Trips down memory lane aren't my style.'

'Why so wary, Rosalind?' he taunted softly. 'I'd almost think I still meant something to you.'

He had always seemed to caress her name. It alarmed her to discover that the sound of it on his lips could still send a quiver tracing down her spine.

'Well, you'd be wrong,' she returned. 'I simply don't wish to talk about old times, as you put it.'

'I thought it might give you a chance to explain what you meant earlier with your comments about Vivienne,' he said, a faintly abrasive note to his voice.

'You may find it hard to believe this,' she replied, wondering for how much longer she could contain her smouldering temper, 'but I no longer care what your relationship with Vivienne is.'

'What makes you think I have a relationship with her at all?'

'Don't lie to me,' she said, not attempting to hide her contempt. 'You were fascinated by her. It was her you wanted from the start, not me.'

'While you wanted Andrew,' he returned drily, 'who's since disappeared from the scene. I find that rather surprising, when he was supposed to be the love of your life.'

Kurt had been that, if he did but know it. She slapped her napkin down on the table, and realised from his quick movement that by doing so she must have come close to upsetting her glass.

'I've had about enough of your sarcasm!' she warned.

Before she could rise from her chair, Kurt's hand closed over her wrist.

'Let go of me!' she demanded, the live warmth of his touch making her pulse quicken. 'I've finished my coffee and I've no desire to sit here being cross-questioned by you any longer.'

'Surely you're not going to disappoint your aunt?' he mocked. 'Doubtless she's spinning out her phone call in the hope that you and I are enjoying a cosy little tête-à-tête.'

'Well, she couldn't be more wrong!' Rosalind replied shortly.

'I take it you're aware she's playing matchmaker?'

'I'd have to be very obtuse not to be!' She resented being held prisoner by him, but only by an undignified tussle did she stand any chance of snatching her wrist free. 'I find it as embarrassing as you do!'

'What makes you think I find it embarrassing?' he drawled lazily. His hand slid down over her wrist, his thumb stroking her knuckles. 'Personally,' he continued, 'I can't see any harm in keeping her happy. You lie so sweetly. I'm sure you could put up a most convincing pretence if you set your mind to it.'

'As you did two years ago?' she said with a rare flash of fire. 'I regret the day I was ever unlucky enough to meet you!'

'Oddly enough, I often look back to that day, too,' he answered, his husky voice dry. He released her wrist, and she heard the faint tinkle of china as his hand idly fingered the handle of his coffee-cup. 'You were wearing a white dress with pale green flowers on it, your hair was in a top-knot and you were prettier than any of the pictures in the gallery.'

Her heart skipped a painful beat as his words took her back two years to their first meeting. She had been a student at the Royal College of Art in London at the time, and she had bumped into him literally and quite by chance one Saturday afternoon at the National Gallery, which housed a number of her favourite paintings.

She'd recently broken up with Andrew, the first real boyfriend she'd ever had. It had been a fairly light-hearted romance, but even so she'd cried when he'd told her he'd met someone else and, having spent so much time with him, had found that their splitting up had left a gap. Wandering round the art gallery was a way of filling it.

She was a great admirer of Turner and she stood gazing at *Sun Rising Through Vapour* for a long time before stepping back consideringly. In doing so she collided with a man's hard chest. A capable hand shot out. As it steadied her she turned to apologise, only to be momentarily stunned by the overwhelming impact the stranger made on her.

Virile power and invincibility were stamped into every line and plane of him. He was tall, well over six feet, and she barely came to his shoulder, making her feel slightly breathless and very feminine.

His hair was black, well cut and smoothly groomed. Two years on she doubted that there was a single thread of grey in it. His eyes were such a vivid and compelling blue that it was like being held in a spotlight. His mouth was sensuous, yet paradoxically masculine. The line of it suggested that he had a quick sense of humour and yet there was a touch of ruthlessness about it that matched the slight sternness of his features, all of which were strong.

'I'm sorry,' she said with a catch of laughter. 'I didn't know you were standing behind me.'

'I was trying to work out what you saw in the picture that you could gaze at it so long,' the man said with a touch of humour. His smile seemed to kick the breath out of her chest for an instant, it was so attractive. 'I like Turner but I wouldn't choose *Sun Rising Through Vapour* to hang in my lounge.'

'Which picture would you choose, then?'

'If it had to be a Turner, *Calais Pier*, but of the Impressionists the artist I like the most is Van Gogh. For me he's way and above all the others.'

Van Gogh was a favourite of hers too. With art forming a link between them they got talking more generally, and Rosalind's first impression of the stranger was borne out. Kurt Wilding was a dynamic and very charismatic man and in his company the afternoon had flown.

But, much as she'd enjoyed the time they'd spent together wandering round the gallery, when he'd suggested they have dinner together one evening she'd smiled and shaken her head. Cinderella-like she'd slipped away from him shortly afterwards. Even on such a short acquaintance Kurt Wilding didn't strike her as the sort of man to give up easily. It seemed safer quietly to vanish than to stay with him any longer.

She didn't realise immediately that she'd left behind the Turner print she'd bought in the gallery gift shop. She was sorry about it but she didn't go back for it in case she collided with Kurt again.

Out on the street, threading her way between the other pedestrians as she headed for the station, she was conscious of a sense of regret and a reluctant feeling that she'd been right simply to slip away.

Kurt's charisma was powerful and it would be a long time before she stopped thinking about him. Each time she did she knew she would wish she had agreed to see him again. But she didn't want to get involved with anyone else so soon after splitting up with Andrew and, in any case, her upbringing meant that she couldn't let herself be picked up casually, however attractive the stranger.

With London being such a big city she was certain she wouldn't run into Kurt twice, yet because he'd made such a striking impression on her she couldn't seem to put him out of her mind. Sitting on her divan bed, her studio flat full of evening sunlight, she found that instead of giving her attention to the series of working drawings she needed for her pottery class the following day she kept picturing Kurt's masculine face, a ridiculous thing to be doing considering that almost a week had elapsed since she had bumped into him.

Absently her pencil began to doodle. Strong patrician features appeared on the page beside her other drawings. The sensual masculine mouth was one she could imagine herself kissing. The wayward thought sent a hot little shiver tracing over her skin and drew her up with a jolt.

Musingly she looked at the portrait she had sketched, a faint blush in her cheeks. She had achieved a striking likeness, her interest in Kurt Wilding only too apparent from the strong, sure lines, the vigorous shading. Annoyed with herself, she tore the sheet off the pad and crumpled it in her hand.

'Now concentrate,' she muttered sternly to herself.

But before she had a chance to begin work on her drawings on a fresh sheet of paper the doorbell rang downstairs.

Her studio flat was on the top floor above a busy doctor's group surgery in what had once been an Edwardian gentleman's house. She'd been lucky to find such good accommodation so attractively priced. All the staff who worked at the practice were friendly, and with two separate doorbells she was seldom troubled by patients wanting one of the doctors after surgery hours.

Setting her sketch-pad aside, she slipped off the bed, a slim half-tamed girl in cotton trousers and a cream knitted top with bracelet sleeves. She ran downstairs and opened the heavy front door, surprised to find Andrew standing outside.

He was young, blond and good-looking, and a fellow student at the Royal College of Art. His father was an architect and his mother an artist. From them he had inherited his creative talent and, like Rosalind, he seemed destined to make a name for himself in the art world of the future.

'Hi,' he began a shade awkwardly.

'Hi,' she returned, wondering why he had called.

'I...thought we might go out for a drink if you're not doing anything this evening,' he ventured.

She realised as she stood at the door talking to him that he wanted them to get back together again. In the time they'd been apart she'd discovered that she wasn't in love with him. She turned down his invitation and then, feeling sorry for him and hoping they could still be friends, she asked him in for coffee.

They were sitting chatting when the doorbell rang.

'Are you expecting someone?' Andrew asked.

'No, I'm not.'

'Then get rid of whoever it is fast,' he said, his smile robbing his words of offence. 'Even if it is over between us, I want you to myself for this evening.'

'OK,' she agreed.

She went downstairs, conscious that she still liked him in a platonic way and glad that their relationship hadn't ended in bitterness. Unsuspectingly she opened the front door, her heart giving a jolt as she saw Kurt standing outside, tall and powerful-looking in a charcoal-grey suit that emphasised the lean, lithe strength of his body.

Parked in the street was a dark green Lotus, presumably his.

'So I've tracked you down at last,' he observed, his vivid blue eyes holding hers.

'What...what are you doing here?' She sounded breathless. Trying to hide the fact that her pulse was suddenly racing, she went on, 'How did you find out my address.'

'With some difficulty, since all I had to go on was your name and the college you're studying at,' he answered with humour. 'What made you disappear that day at the gallery? I couldn't believe it when I turned round and you were gone.'

'I...' Her confusion, she realised, was almost an answer in itself. Pulling herself together, she said, challenged by his masculine presence, 'I didn't disappear. We bumped into each other by chance. Then we parted. That's all there was to it.'

'Really?' he questioned softly. The combination of his husky voice and devastating smile made her heart lurch. Perturbed by the vibrations of attraction between them, she was shatteringly conscious of the strength and determination beneath his charm. 'The impression I got was that you bolted because you were afraid I was going to talk you into having dinner with me.'

She blushed and was immediately cross with herself because it confirmed what he'd said was true.

'I don't accept dates from men I don't know,' she told him.

'Then ask me in and we'll get acquainted.'

'I thought I'd made it clear, Mr Wilding——'

'The name's Kurt, the same as it was last Saturday,' he cut across her with gentle mockery. 'And by the way, you forgot this.'

He handed her the Turner print she'd left behind in the gallery gift shop.

'Thank you,' she murmured. 'It... it was nice of you to bring it round.'

'My pleasure.'

As he spoke his eyes travelled over her again, noting her gamine slimness and the softness of her burnished hair that fell loose around her shoulders. When his eyes returned to her face they smiled at her, and such was the force of his charisma that she found herself smiling back, albeit shyly.

'Well, thank you again,' she said, on the point of saying goodbye when Andrew's voice made her glance round.

'Rosalind?' Coming down the stairs, he took in the tall stranger standing just beyond the doorway. 'Who's this?' he demanded, sliding his hands into the pockets of his jeans as he joined her.

Steely blue eyes looked Andrew up and down, as the man assessed the boy. It was plain he was bemused by what Rosalind saw in him.

'Kurt Wilding,' he said, identifying himself before Rosalind had the chance to introduce him.

'The architect, Kurt Wilding?' Andrew said. With his father in the same profession, the name clearly meant something to him.

'The same,' Kurt agreed. 'And who are you?'

'I'm Rosalind's boyfriend.'

Kurt's mouth curled a little with contempt.

'So you're the guy who stood her up for someone else,' he observed.

Andrew flushed angrily. He had always been impulsive and, afraid he was going to get into a fight he couldn't possibly win, Rosalind took a step forward. But her intervention was unnecessary. Andrew clearly knew he wasn't of the calibre to confront a man like Kurt.

Turning to Rosalind, he said in a bitter undertone, 'No wonder you wouldn't come out for a drink with me. Why didn't you tell me you'd met someone else instead of playing me for a fool?'

'I didn't!' she protested, only to have Kurt cut in,

'Don't let us keep you.' His tone as he addressed Andrew was amiable. It was the chilliness in his eyes that cancelled it out.

Intimidated, Andrew brushed past her, in a hurry to be gone.

'Andrew, wait!' She rushed after him, conscious of Kurt watching her, a dark eyebrow cocked in lazy appraisal.

She was fairly burning up with temper she was so furious with him. But at the moment her first consideration was Andrew. Catching hold of him by the sleeve, she began, 'It's not the way it looks...'

'It didn't take long for you to find someone else, did it?' he bit back, prising her fingers from his jacket before striding off down the street.

'Andrew!' she called desperately, about to run after him when a hand closed on her arm.

'Let him go,' Kurt ordered negligently.

She spun round to face him, a slender, outraged fury.

'How dare you? How dare you treat Andrew that way?' she blazed.

'What way?'

'You used what I told you that day at the gallery to make it look as if... as if...' She broke off, floundering, anger prompting her to begin a sentence that for some reason she couldn't finish.

'As if the two of us are lovers?' Kurt completed the sentence for her, the sensual base notes of his voice sending electricity flickering along her nerves.

'You've got a damned nerve,' she stormed. Her gaze followed Andrew as, without a backward glance, he rounded the corner. It was obvious he thought she hadn't been honest with him, that she and Kurt were involved with each other. Maybe he even thought she'd asked him in for coffee just so she could slap him down all the harder. He was bitter and angry and she knew he'd never listen to her even if she tried to explain. Almost in tears because she hated hurting anyone, she went on, 'Because of you now I'll never be able to make up with Andrew!'

'Did you want to make up with him?' Kurt asked calmly while his eyes, arrestingly blue and hawkishly keen, probed hers.

'Since you've sent him away, it's academic, isn't it?' she said fiercely, fumbling in her sleeve for a handkerchief and failing to find one.

Kurt reached into the pocket of his jacket and handed her his own.

'Whereas the subject of you and me is anything but academic,' he told her.

Angrily she took his pristine white handkerchief, wishing she dared slap his face. Forcing herself to breathe deeply, she tried to quell the riotous feelings inside her. What was there about Kurt Wilding, that he made her react so violently? First she had taken flight from him. Now she longed to hit him.

'What's that supposed to mean?' she asked, glaring at him with eyes that glistened with tears and yet were full of sparks.

'We'll talk about it inside,' he answered, his patient yet faintly mocking inflexion implying that she knew full well what he meant. 'I suggest you ask me in,' he replied evenly. Despite the amusement that played around the masculine line of his mouth, she sensed the steel behind his words. 'Unless, that is, you want to give your neighbours still more to gossip about.'

She dragged her gaze away from his and saw what he'd been quick to observe, but she had failed to notice. A shadow moved behind the net curtains of the house next door. There was no doubt they were being spied on from that quarter, while the little boy from across the road had stopped riding his bike and was watching their altercation with interest.

'What are you, some kind of salesman, that you're so good at bullying your way in where you're not wanted?' she asked as reluctantly she led the way indoors.

To her intense annoyance his reaction to her scathing remark wasn't at all what she had expected. Far from rising to it, he laughed, a very masculine sound.

'I thought your ex had just vouched that I am what I claimed to be.'

'A famous architect with no manners!' she summarised as, with her slim shoulders very squared, she walked ahead of him up the stairs.

It was the second of her verbal arrows that failed to find its target. Rather as a lion might tolerate the mischievous pranks of a cub, he ignored her gibe. His step lithe and silent, he followed her into her flat and looked about him. Though Rosalind had had no hand in its decoration since the studio flat was a furnished one, she was responsible for the welcoming feel it had.

There was a bright pink geranium on the small pine table that stood in the centre of the room and another on the windowsill. Cheerful patchwork cushions were scattered on the divan, while her photographs and books, which lined the shelves, made the room an interesting one.

'So this is where you live,' he said, his inflexion suggesting that he liked her style.

She remained where she was, just inside the door. Dark and swarthy, Kurt seemed to make her flat shrink in size, such was the power of his personality. Far too conscious of the mercurial rise of her pulse every time her gaze was ensnared by his, she preferred to keep the distance of the room between them.

'Why did you go to the trouble of finding out my address?' she challenged, still furious with him over the way he had sent Andrew away.

'You know why.'

'No, I don't,' she lied, far too unsettled by the awareness between them to admit openly to its existence. 'How could I?'

'Then I'll spell it out. I took the trouble to find out where you live because I wanted to see you again.'

The calmly spoken statement made her heartbeat quicken. She wasn't sure how to reply. Fresh out of one relationship, she wasn't ready to get involved immediately in another, and especially not with a man who instinct warned her would have the ability to create havoc with her emotions if she allowed him into her life.

Defiantly she answered, 'You're wasting your time, Mr Wilding. As you can see, I already have a boyfriend.'

'Your ex?' he mocked before informing her, 'I never waste my time. Now how about offering me some coffee?'

'I've no intention of offering you coffee!'

'And you say I've no manners,' he gibed gently.

She glared at him, noting in spite of herself the way the sunlight gleamed on his thick black hair.

'I'd like you to leave,' she said.

'You're very wilful. Now stop behaving like a child.'

'Or what?' she challenged with a flash of spirit.

He came towards her, and tilted up her chin. His gaze lingered on the fullness of her lips, making her pulse quicken dizzily.

'I liked the girl I met at the gallery who was so warm and lively very much,' he drawled. 'Now, how do you suggest I summon her back.'

Her breath seemed trapped in her chest.

'Don't... don't you dare kiss me,' she whispered in a panic.

'Then make me some coffee,' Kurt smiled, watching the apricot blush that had come into her cheeks, and which made her even prettier.

She went over to the tiny sink and began to fill the kettle, indignation taking over from her initial flustered climb-down. Just who did he think he was, demanding that she make him coffee? Angrily she spooned instant coffee into two cups. And just what was he doing here, anyway? Her conscious self declared that she had no idea, while her subconscious self knew perfectly.

The magnetism that had pulsed between them that day in the gallery was there in all its force again now. It was small wonder that she was panicking. She'd never met anyone with Kurt's sexual charisma before. The other men she knew were really boys, at the most a couple of years older than she was. But there was nothing remotely boyish about the man who was prowling about her small flat almost as though he owned it.

'Do you take your coffee black or white?' she asked in a tone which suggested that whichever he asked for, he'd get the opposite.

'Well, well.'

His lazily amused comment made her turn to see what prompted it. She blushed hotly as she saw that in his hand was the sketch she had made of him, which he had smoothed out to examine.

'Give me that,' she demanded.

His eyes lifted from the sketch to meet hers.

'Very flattering,' he drawled.

Discomfited, she disagreed with as much coolness as she could muster, 'I wouldn't have said so. It's an accurate likeness. Your features are craggy rather than handsome.'

'I meant it's flattering to know I was on your mind,' he said.

She could hardly deny that. 'You... you have an interesting face,' she faltered.

She turned back to switch off the kettle that had started to boil. Aware in every inch of her that Kurt was advancing towards her, she poured out the water, her hands trembling so much that she spilt most of it in his saucer.

Kurt took hold of her by the shoulders, compelling her to face him. She looked up into his eyes, almost mesmerised by their blueness. Through her thin knitted top she could feel the warmth of his hands on her skin. Not only did she feel suddenly weak, but her pulse was faster.

'Kurt, please...' she managed in a whisper, beseeching him to give her more space.

His eyes drank in the lovely lines of her face while she stared up at him, the awareness between them so strong that it was like a haze filling the room.

'Have dinner with me next week,' he said finally, his smile sending a delicious shiver along her spine.

'I... I work late at college Tuesdays, Thursdays and Fridays,' she said, in one last bid to remain aloof from his magnetism.

'Wednesday is fine,' he answered mockingly. 'I'll call for you at eight.'

As he spoke he reached out his hand to caress the line of her jaw. She caught her breath at his touch and a raw flame seemed to flicker in the depths of his eyes as he noted her response to him.

He moved closer and, unable to make even the slightest sound of protest, she watched as he bent his head, the strong lines of his face blurring in the instant before his lips brushed hers in the lightest of kisses.

'Make sure you're ready on time,' he said softly, his husky voice as sensual as his gaze.

She was devastated to realise that she wanted him to kiss her again, only more deeply this time. Kurt was self-assured, tough, charming and experienced. Every instinct told her she was out of her depth with him and she should put up every barrier against him that she could think of. Except already it was too late.

'All right, Wednesday,' she agreed in a whisper.

CHAPTER THREE

'WHEN you vanished that day at the National Gallery I suppose I should have seen it as a forecast of your future behaviour.' Kurt's sardonic comment recalled Rosalind from her reverie.

'Instinct told me to beware of strangers,' she returned, 'and I should have backed my instincts all the way. Though I didn't in fact vanish on any other occasion, unless you're referring to my coming back home to Madeira. And by then, if you remember, our relationship was over.'

'Very much over,' he agreed drily.

'What a complete romantic I was,' she said with a short laugh. 'I actually hoped you'd be supportive.'

'Did you?' he said. 'Well, we all have our illusions, I suppose.'

Hers at the time being that he would tell her he still loved her, that they would come to terms with the dreadful blow together.

'I'm staggered at how hard you are,' she said. 'if you'd loved me...'

She broke off, furious that she was allowing him to make her feel such a torment of hurt even after all this time.

'How long did you mean to keep it a secret?' he demanded. 'Or did you mean not to tell me at all?'

'I can't see any purpose in this conversation,' she said, screening all the pain inside her with coldness.

'Perhaps you can't but I'm curious,' he returned. 'I'd like an answer.'

There was an edge of steel in his voice despite its evenness and responding to it she retorted, 'Of course I'd have told you! I'd even have understood it making some difference.' Ironically, when she'd learned that she was suffering from a rare eye disease that was hereditary she'd steeled herself to relinquishing Kurt's love, knowing that any child she had would be at risk of going blind. Shattered by the diagnosis, she'd intended telling Kurt he was free from any promises he'd made to her. And all the time she'd hoped desperately that he'd say her blindness couldn't change the way he felt about her. Instead, the moment he knew, Kurt had made it very plain he no longer wished to marry her. Bitterly she went on, 'What I didn't expect was that you'd be so heartless!'

The slight scrape of his shoe on the stone told that he had leant back into his chair, his long legs staking out a claim on the patio.

'You do the wronged act very well,' he observed with a touch of cynicism.

'Just what are you blaming me for?' she demanded and then guessed suddenly. Since Leber's disease was hereditary, presumably he thought she'd known all along that it ran in her family. Except that she hadn't known. There was no trace of it on her father's side of the family, and since her mother had been adopted and had never known who her real parents were, the medical history of her family remained a blank. Coldly but calmly she stated, 'I couldn't tell you at the beginning for the simple reason that I didn't know myself.'

'When did you find out?' Kurt questioned.

His tone, that was marginally less abrasive, suggested that he was inclined to believe her.

'While you were in Canada,' she said. 'It was as big a shock to me as it obviously was to you.'

'Are you telling me you honestly didn't know until then?' he persisted.

'What sort of person do you think I am?' she retorted. 'Do you think I could have gone ahead and married you knowing——'

He cut in, 'According to Vivienne, that was exactly what you intended doing.'

'And of course you'd take her word against mine!' she said.

Kurt didn't reply immediately. Unable to see his expression, she had to rely on her imagination in order to visualise his face. The atmosphere that was dangerously charged with tension told her that his dark brows were drawn together in a frown.

'It would have helped if you'd told me all this before,' he said drily at last.

'Told you what?' she was about to ask when footsteps heralded her aunt's return to the patio.

'I'm sorry that took so long,' Julia began as she sat down again. 'But I'm sure the two of you found plenty to chat about.'

'We were discussing old times,' Kurt said, his subtle mockery directed at Rosalind.

'I'm sorry I interrupted, then,' her aunt laughed.

'You haven't,' Kurt assured her. 'It's time anyway I drove over to Camacha to take a look at your building plot. I've sat over lunch longer than I meant to.'

'The keys to the Mercedes are on the table in the hall,' Julia said. 'Or would you like me to come with you?'

'No, I'm sure I'll find the site without any problem,' he told her. 'I've got the deeds you gave me.'

Intent on throwing them together, Julia suggested to Rosalind, 'Perhaps you'd like to go along with Kurt.'

'I'm quite sure he doesn't need me to hold his hand!' she retorted.

Kurt's laugh acknowledged that he was amused by her reply. 'I wouldn't say that,' he drawled mockingly. He got to his feet. 'I'll see you later.'

As his firm steps faded Rosalind began, 'Julia, you will have to stop this!'

'Stop what?'

'This blatant matchmaking.'

'What makes you think I'm matchmaking?' Julia asked, feigning innocence.

'It's very obvious. I should have guessed last night what you were up to when you suddenly sprang it on me that you'd engaged Kurt as your architect.'

'I'm sorry I didn't think to mention to you before that I'd invited him,' Julia said. 'I was so wrapped up with my plans for making my home here on Madeira that it honestly slipped my mind.'

'Did it?' Rosalind was lightly sceptical.

'Oh, very well,' Julia abandoned her pretence. 'Maybe I am hoping that you and Kurt will patch up whatever it is that went wrong between the two of you.'

'I may be blind, but I'm still quite capable of managing my own life. There is a phone service on the island,' Rosalind reminded her aunt, 'and I can always ask someone to write a letter for me if there's any need. If I'd wanted to see Kurt again I'd have contacted him myself.'

'I've said I'm sorry,' Julia defended herself. 'Though if you don't still love Kurt I can't see why you care that I've invited him. And if you do still love him, then isn't it worth a try to sort things out?'

'You don't understand!'

'No, frankly I don't.'

'Julia, there's no chance that Kurt and I will ever get back together. So please don't try to force us into each other's company because I mean to stay out of his way as much as possible the whole time he's here.'

'Why?' her aunt demanded.

'Because he's the last man on earth I want to have anything more to do with!'

'I didn't realise you felt so strongly.' Julia sounded surprised.

'Well, I do,' Rosalind confirmed.

There was a pause and then Julia said, 'Will you explain one thing for me?'

'What's that?' Rosalind asked.

'Ever since I first contacted Kurt about the new house I've been puzzled by something he said to me. He thought you were married. I couldn't understand why he was so surprised when I said that you weren't. Where did he get the idea from?'

'I wanted him to think there was someone else,' Rosalind said, her voice oddly cramped.

'I see,' Julia said, her tone indicating that she was no nearer to understanding what had happened between them than she had been before.

'Did...did Kurt ask anything else about me when you talked?' Rosalind wanted to know.

'He asked if you still saw anything of someone called...' Her aunt broke off, searching for the name.

'Andrew,' Rosalind supplied quietly.

'That's right, Andrew,' Julia agreed. She added reflectively, 'Whatever happened in the past, it's clear Kurt still finds you very attractive. You're laughing together, reminiscing together, and I haven't imagined the sparks flying between you. I think——'

'And I'm telling you you're wrong,' Rosalind cut in. 'Now, please,' she appealed, 'will you stop interfering?'

'I wouldn't have to if you'd just use a little common sense,' her aunt replied patiently. 'Kurt's attractive, successful and good company. You don't find men like that growing on trees, especially...'

'Especially when you happen to be blind?' Rosalind guessed the ending to the sentence.

'That wasn't what I was going to say!' her aunt protested. 'I don't know why you're so sensitive about being blind when it comes to boyfriends.'

'I'm not,' Rosalind insisted.

'Well, I think you are,' her aunt disagreed. 'According to Bernard you've turned down dates with at least two young men who'd have been only too pleased to go out with you.'

'I didn't realise Dad was so anxious to get me married off!' Rosalind said.

Her droll humour was wasted on her aunt.

'Of course he's not anxious to get you married off,' Julia answered. 'The fact that you don't want to get involved with anyone didn't even seem to have struck him until I asked him whether there had been anyone special since Kurt.'

'I don't want anyone special,' Rosalind said.

There was a pause and then Julia asserted, 'What I can't understand is that with every other facet of life you refuse to let your blindness make any difference. You've carried on with your work, despite all the problems of learning to see with your hands. So why this mental block when it comes to romance?'

'How many men do you know who'd want to be saddled with a blind wife?'

'That's a very cynical attitude!'

'Perhaps I've met some very cynical men,' Rosalind said quietly. She was thinking of Kurt.

It was early evening before he returned from Camacha, by which time she was in her room getting changed. She fingered the apricot short-sleeved blouse she had chosen to wear. Teamed with silk charmeuse trousers and a matching jacket, her outfit was casual and yet had a kind of Thirties-style glamour which suited her.

She hoped it was right for her dinner date. With her being blind, her only mirror was the honesty of someone who could see, and had Julia not been downstairs talking to Kurt in the drawing-room she would have asked her aunt's opinion. As it was, she took the decision to back her own judgement.

The gold bracelets on her wrist jangled prettily as she brushed her thick coppery hair. She left it loose to frame her face and them sprayed her pulse-points with Eternity. The scent of narcissus combined with the fragrance of sandalwood to give the very feminine perfume a lightness and subtlety that made it one of her favourites.

She checked the time, a faint furrow of indecision appearing between her brows as she did so. Manuel would be calling for her very shortly. It was tempting to find a reason to linger upstairs until he arrived and then to go straight out of the house. On the other hand, she didn't want it to be obvious to Kurt that she was doing her best to keep out of his way. A slightly defiant set to her mouth, she opted to put in a brief appearance in the drawing-room.

She went downstairs and took her white cane out of the umbrella stand in the hall. She knew Manuel would be only too willing to place a guiding hand at the small of her back, but endless gentle pushes and a flow of would-be helpful words made her feel nervous. They were distractions which could easily make her stumble. Her cane gave her a sense of security and allowed her to be independent.

She entered the drawing-room to hear the rustling of papers being handled and Julia saying, 'These sketches will give you an idea of what I have in mind.' Her aunt, who was sitting on the sofa, glanced up to greet her. 'I'm just telling Kurt about the type of house I want built.'

'And I'm trying to explain to your aunt,' Kurt said, 'that, having visited the site this afternoon to make a preliminary survey, I can see that there are certain constraints to be taken into account.' There was a shading of tolerant masculine amusement in his voice.

'What sort of constraints?' Rosalind asked as she sat down in one of the armchairs.

She propped her cane up alongside her. It was crazy, but even such a casual exchange with Kurt was enough to set her heart beating erratically. It seemed a reflex response to him that time couldn't alter.

'Well, for one thing, as I expect you know,' he answered, 'Madeira has very strict planning laws. Then there's the slope of the land to consider. It shelves very steeply. Getting the foundations down for anything more than a bungalow is going to be difficult.'

'I can see I'm going to have to resign myself to tearing these sketches up,' Julia laughed.

'Not at all,' Kurt insisted. A smile in his voice, he joked, 'Just resign yourself to having them modified a little.'

Reluctantly Rosalind had to applaud his charm. Kurt might be hard and ruthless, but he also knew how to be suave, disarming and extremely diplomatic. She remembered his telling her once that only a fraction of his work was truly creative in the generally accepted meaning of the word. The rest of his time was spent doing site surveys, pulling rank on building foremen, cajoling planning committees and negotiating over contracts.

She didn't doubt that her aunt's typically unfeasible ideas would be set to one side. And when Julia saw what Rosalind knew would be a brilliant set of plans and drawings she would be so delighted she would be quite happy to abandon her own notions in favour of Kurt's.

Her thoughts were interrupted by the sound of a car drawing up outside.

'That will be Manuel,' she said, pleased that he was so prompt.

She would have got to her feet but Julia forestalled her by announcing, 'As it's Maria's night off, I'll go and let him in.'

She went out of the drawing-room. The faint prickling that stirred at the back of Rosalind's neck warned her that Kurt's gaze was on her, while her imagination told her that it was detached and sardonic. His tone when he spoke seemed to confirm her assumption.

'Manuel hasn't booked a table at Reid's, I suppose,' he said. 'It would be ironic if we ended up at the same hotel this evening.'

She caught his meaning perfectly, but, choosing to pretend that she hadn't, she answered calmly, 'I don't see why.'

Kurt didn't contradict her. It was his faintly exhaled breath of cynical amusement which told her he knew full well she was bluffing. Though Julia was totally wrong about her feelings for him, she had to concede that her aunt had been correct about the sparks in the atmosphere when she and Kurt were together. Telling herself to ignore them, she leaned back in her armchair and crossed her legs. There was a sudden clatter.

'What was that?' she asked, starting visibly.

'Your cane's fallen down, that's all,' he informed her, before asking, 'Do you always start at any sudden sound?'

'Not usually,' she answered.

Normally she wouldn't have jumped. Her cane had become so much a part of her life that she knew its every sound. Her reaction was a measure of how tense she was because of Kurt's presence.

'Then you must be on edge for some reason,' he said.

'So would you be if you couldn't see to identify the cause of a sound,' she parried, certain he was about to make some gibe.

He surprised her by merely agreeing, 'True.'

She heard him rise from the sofa. Her heartbeat speeding up in response to his approach, she insisted quickly, 'It's all right. I can find it.'

She moved her foot in an arc, intending when she located it to bend down and pick it up. But the toe that slid over the marble floor failed to make contact with it.

Her inner radar told her that Kurt was almost on top of her. She abandoned her search as he stooped to the left of her armchair, retrieving the cane for her.

'Here,' he said, putting it into her hand and closing her fingers round it with his own.

'Thank you,' she murmured unwillingly, the pulse that beat at the base of her throat the only indication of how much his nearness disturbed her.

Twice now he had touched her. It mystified her that, when she knew that his whole attitude towards her disability was one of hardness, the message the touch of his hand conveyed was one of caring strength.

When he had handed her cane to her she expected him to move away. Instead he remained where he was. With nothing save greyness in front of her eyes, she could neither read his expression, nor guess what was going through his mind as he stood for a moment studying her.

Then his firm tread restored a distance between them. Able to breathe more easily, she heard him say as he resumed their conversation, 'So where's Manuel taking you this evening?'

'To the Sheraton, I expect,' she said. 'The food's very good there, but the atmosphere is more informal; it suits me better. You'll have to dress for dinner at Reid's, but I don't suppose you'll dine much before eight-thirty so you've heaps of time to change.'

A quizzical note in his husky voice, Kurt asked, 'How do you know what I'm wearing?'

'Your sleeve brushed my arm as you handed me my cane,' she explained. She realised with surprise that for the first time they were actually talking, not sparring in a veiled sort of way. 'The weave of the cloth wasn't fine enough to be a dinner-jacket.'

'You're quite a detective,' Kurt laughed, impressed.

She didn't want to share a joke with him. Any reminder of the rapport there had once been between them was painful, yet even so her lips curved into a smile.

'Of course, you always liked playing the detective,' he went on. 'Agatha Christie, wasn't it, that you especially enjoyed?'

'She still is a favourite of mine,' Rosalind said, in an attempt to keep the conversation focused on the present.

'Do you remember the evening we went to St Martin's Theatre to see *The Mouse Trap*?' Kurt asked, apparently unaware that the last thing she wanted to talk about was the happy times they had shared together.

'Yes,' she said quietly, giving nothing away.

'You'd guessed who'd done it almost before the end of scene one!'

She was forced to laugh in spite of herself.

'Did I ruin it for you, telling you who I suspected?' she asked.

'If anything it added to the suspense. I wanted to know if you were right, and of course you were. I was most impressed.'

She smiled and he commented, 'We seem to be doing slightly better.'

She heard the click of his lighter and as cigarette smoke drifted towards her she said, 'I...I'm sorry? I don't follow you.'

'At lunch the atmosphere was decidedly cool.'

His words broke the fragile rapport that had been building between them.

'What did you expect after the way we broke up?' she asked, hurt all the more because for an instant while they had been talking she had forgotten the callous way he had treated her. 'We hardly parted as friends.'

'No, there'd been too much between us for that,' he said, a reflective note to his voice.

Since Kurt had been in love with someone else the whole time, she could scarcely take his remark as sincere.

'Am I to deduce from that that you actually have some regrets?' Her cool irony was prompted by a desire to ease some of the anger that was rising up inside her with their conversation.

'Odd, isn't it,' Kurt observed, 'how you and I can't be alone together for five minutes before one of us mentions the past and we start sniping at each other?'

His implication was that, as she'd been the one to raise the subject, she was the one with the regrets about their broken engagement.

'Are you suggesting we call a truce?' she answered in the same tone as before, her chin lifting.

'No, I'm going one better. I'm suggesting we try to be friends.'

There was no trace of sarcasm in his voice and, feeling strangely as though he had suddenly cut the ground from beneath her, she challenged, 'Do you think it's possible?'

'You don't accept an olive branch too graciously, do you?' he returned.

She coloured slightly. He was confusing her and she hated him for it. She felt safer when they were sparring, when she could forget the closeness they had once shared.

'I—I'll accept it on one condition,' she said, suddenly deciding.

'What condition's that?' he asked.

'That we agree we won't discuss the past.'

'I can understand you'd prefer that,' he commented.

Not sure what to make of his reply, she began, 'Does that mean you accept?'

'No, it doesn't,' came the answer.

There was something implacable in his flinty tone.

'Then there's no point...' she flared, feeling she couldn't stand to be reminded at every turn of why he'd rejected her.

It was Julia's interruption that made her check her flow of words. A heavier step, Manuel's, accompanied her footsteps. Breathing in deeply, Rosalind calmed her temper. She couldn't understand Kurt. How did he think they could be friends when the past was always between them? And yet she'd been ready to agree to his suggestion. It worried her because it showed that, whatever her feelings for him, she still wasn't immune to his magnetism.

'Kurt,' Julia began brightly, 'I'd like you to meet Manuel Pereiros, an old friend of ours.'

'Not all that old!' Manuel joked in protest. 'At least I don't feel it this evening.'

'Now you know I didn't mean it that way,' Julia laughed. 'I meant my brother's known you so long you're almost one of the family.'

'How do you do?' There was nothing in Kurt's voice to suggest that he and Rosalind had been matching words only seconds before.

'I understand you're here to draw up the plans for Julia's new house,' Manuel said as the two men shook hands.

'That's the idea.'

'Well, I hope you have a very pleasant stay at the same time,' Manuel said. 'It's so easy to relax on Madeira. Do you like swimming or tennis?' he asked conversationally.

'I enjoy both,' Kurt told him. 'Maybe we could fix up a game later in the week.'

'Fine. I'll look forward to it.'

For a brief moment, despite the amiable nature of the exchange, Rosalind had the curious impression of the two men squaring off against each other. Abandoning the notion as illogical, she said, 'It's a pity it's such a long drive to Porto Moniz. The sea-water pools that are built into the lava rocks there are lovely.'

'Is that an offer to come with me?' Kurt asked with a trace of mockery.

She had simply been making an observation, as he knew perfectly well, but before she could answer her aunt put in, pleased, 'That's a splendid idea!'

Rosalind's temperature rose with annoyance, but, very much in control of herself, she said nothing. To show that she was nettled would merely add to Kurt's satisfaction.

'Well, Rosalind,' Manuel announced, 'if we're to be on time we'd better be going.'

She nodded, only too glad to get to her feet. It might be over between her and Kurt, but her constant awareness of his virile appeal and the static in the atmosphere was becoming more and more of a strain on her. If she was to continue to respond to his mockery with a pretence of calm she needed a respite from his company.

'How are you making out?' Manuel asked her as they drove away from the *quinta*, his meaning obvious.

'I'm making out fine,' she answered, with rather more bravado than sincerity.

The truth was, she was wondering how on earth she was going to get through the week that lay ahead when all the stormy emotions she had believed she had dealt with were simmering not far beneath the surface.

In an effort not to allow her skirmishes with Kurt to ruin her evening, she tried to put him out of her mind. It helped that Manuel was such a companionable person to be with.

Rosalind chatted to him easily as they sped along the main road, her light-hearted remarks drawing from him several appreciative barks of laughter. The landscape in the evening sunlight was glorious. Hay formed ribbons of gold among the patchwork of vineyards, fields and cultivated terraces. Blue and white agapanthus grew in profusion by the wayside and, with every house covered with some kind of climbing plant, the suburbs of Funchal were as ablaze with colour as was the countryside.

The city, which was built around the harbour, rose steeply up the encircling hills. Portuguese colonial architecture combined with open-air cafés, noisy traffic and pavements shaded with palm trees and bright with cacti and hibiscus to make Funchal a fascinating mixture of old-world charm and modern bustle.

Mindful that Rosalind felt self-conscious eating out, Manuel had chosen, not a hotel as she had supposed, but a small and delightfully friendly restaurant close to the city centre. With its vine-covered terrace and rustic décor it had a simple elegance. Piano music, the tinkle of glass and the muted buzz of conversation from the other tables created a relaxing ambience and the evening seemed to fly.

They were lingering over coffee and liqueurs when Manuel said, 'A penny for them?'

'What?' she asked, startled, as his voice cut into her thoughts. She gave a rueful little laugh. 'I'm sorry. I was listening to the music.'

'"These Foolish Things",' Manuel identified the tune.

'Yes,' she agreed with a wry smile.

Manuel studied her quizzically for an instant before observing, obviously having guessed that the tune reminded her of Kurt, 'You've been very lively and engaging company this evening and, furthermore, not once have you mentioned your ex-fiancé.'

'Why should I mention him?' she said with a slight shrug. 'He happens to be working for Julia at present. End of story.'

'Or, story to be continued,' Manuel replied. 'A tough customer, our Kurt Wilding. I'm very glad duels are no longer legal.'

'Duels? What are you talking about?' she asked with puzzled amusement.

'When Kurt suggested we have a game of tennis some time in the week I had the feeling that had it been earlier times he'd have challenged me to a duel with pistols at dawn,' Manuel explained. He gave a dry chuckle. 'I also have the unpleasant hunch his aim would be deadly accurate.'

'Why should Kurt want to challenge you to a duel?' she demanded.

'Because he regards me as a rival.'

'You have a lively imagination,' she said. She smiled a shade wanly. 'It's extremely flattering what you're saying, but I can assure you Kurt has no interest in me whatsoever.'

'You think not?' Manuel replied. 'I'm not so sure. If you're holding out on him, my dear, my advice to you is; beware.'

'What do you mean?' she asked.

'Let's just say I've been doing some thinking,' he answered. 'You broke off your engagement to Kurt two years ago and you were diagnosed as suffering from Leber's disease two years ago. Rather coincidental, don't you agree?'

Her hand, which rested beside her liqueur glass, began to toy with its stem. Wishing there were some way of dealing with the ache beneath her ribs that surfaced with every reminder of the past, she said quietly, 'Very coincidental. You've guessed, haven't you?'

'I think so,' he replied. 'I think you wouldn't marry Kurt because you knew you were going blind.

And if I've guessed, I'm wondering how long it will be before he does.'

The reality was so very different from what Manuel was surmising that his words seemed to tear open all the wounds to her heart anew. Yet on the surface she handled it well. Her voice remarkably even, she teased, hiding the brimming pain inside her, 'You're a romantic, Manuel.'

'And so are you. To relinquish Kurt because you knew you were losing your sight would be just the sort of noble thing you'd do.'

'I'm afraid I can't take the credit for that,' she said, and silently prayed that he would now leave the subject alone.

She didn't want to have to tell him that Kurt had never loved her, that from the very beginning there had been someone else. It wasn't only pride that made her not want to talk about the callous way he had treated her. It was also a curious reluctance to show him in such a damning light.

'You're surely not saying...?' Manuel began, a frown in his voice as though he couldn't credit it.

'Kurt wanted children,' she said quietly, 'and since Leber's disease is hereditary we... we decided it would be better if we didn't marry.'

It was the word 'we' that was a lie. Her mind went back two years. What a fool she had been not to realise that it was Vivienne Lloyd whom Kurt loved, and not her. She had been so naïve. The fact that she and Kurt had just become engaged after a whirlwind courtship and that Vivienne was married meant that it had never occurred to her to see the other woman as a rival.

She remembered the warm June evening Kurt had invited the Lloyds round to his house for drinks.

It had been the weekend before he had had to fly out to Toronto in connection with a new cultural centre that was being built there.

The memories were so vivid that she could recall in detail his Regency house fronting on to the river at Marlow, the wisp of a jade silk dress she had been wearing. Vivienne had looked slim and stunning in a turquoise dress with a black motif.

The colour had been chosen because of her eyes. It matched them perfectly and enhanced her shining ash-blonde hair that was swept off her face into a chic twist. Around her neck was a long string of turquoise beads. Seated a short distance away from such sophisticated elegance, Rosalind felt painfully *ingénue* and unadorned.

They had sat outside on the paved terrace sipping aperitifs. Bradley Lloyd was a solidly built, imperturbable man with a good sense of humour and Rosalind had taken to him at once.

She had feathered a finger across her lashes as they sat chatting while Vivienne stood leaning against the balustrade talking to Kurt.

'Is the sun in your eyes?' Bradley asked. 'Move your chair round a little.'

'No, it's not that,' she answered. 'I don't know what it is, but my vision doesn't seem as sharp as it should be.' With no idea that her blurred sight was anything to worry about, she made light of it. 'I'll have to make an appointment to see an optician. I expect I'll be told I need glasses so I hope there's no truth in Dorothy Parker's little couplet.'

'None whatsoever,' Bradley said with an amused smile. 'I can assure you, men make passes at girls who wear glasses all the time.'

Vivienne's gaze flickered to them as she inclined her head to accept a light from Kurt. It was because Rosalind was conscious of the other woman's cool glance that she happened to overhear a fragment of their conversation.

'I never thought you'd be guilty of cradle-snatching, Kurt.'

Rosalind didn't catch his reply, but whatever it was it drew a ripple of laughter in response. She told herself she was being stupidly sensitive to feel vaguely disquieted by the rapport Vivienne and Kurt obviously shared. Kurt loved her and she loved him. There was nothing and no one that could ever come between them.

CHAPTER FOUR

THE Lloyds had left and Rosalind and Kurt were on their own in his spacious lounge when he asked, 'What did you think of Vivienne?'

'She's very beautiful.'

Kurt slanted a glance at her,

'Does that mean you like her or that you don't?' he questioned with a touch of masculine humour.

'What makes you ask?' she hedged.

'Curiosity,' he said. 'I don't think she has many women friends.'

Rosalind could believe that. Vivienne had struck her as very much a man's woman.

'Have you known the Lloyds a long time?' she asked.

'The three of us were at Cambridge together.'

'So Vivienne's a qualified architect too.'

'No, she was a philosophy, politics and economics student,' Kurt said.

Rosalind thought how beguiling and decorative Vivienne had looked as she sat on the terrace. It had been her sharp comments on current affairs which had shown that behind her cool turquoise eyes was an equally sharp mind.

'So that was how you met her—through Bradley,' she surmised.

'No, it was the other way round. Bradley met her through me.'

The implication of his statement hit her like a blow.

'You mean she was your girlfriend before...'

'Before she was his?' Kurt guessed the end of her faltering sentence. 'Yes, she was.'

There was something final about his answer and Rosalind flashed him a glance, trying to read his expression and conscious of a pang of unease. Immediately she talked herself out of it, determined she wasn't going to be the sort of insecure woman who was jealous of every previous relationship her fiancé had ever entered into.

Kurt was attractive, dynamic, amusing and wordly-wise. There must have been a lot of women in his life. Vivienne happened to have been one of them. And the fact that he and Bradley had remained friends ever since university days was surely evidence that Kurt didn't covet his wife in any way.

Vivienne's phone call to her the following Tuesday also allayed her fears.

'I thought you were probably missing Kurt and so I'd give you a ring this evening,' she began with a little rush of charm. 'Have you heard from him yet?'

'Yes, he called me from Toronto yesterday.'

'And I suppose when he gets back you'll start thinking about your wedding plans,' Vivienne said. A ripple of humour in her voice, she went on, 'You two certainly don't believe in long engagements. I couldn't believe it when Kurt said you'd actually fixed the date in July already. Are you going to have the wedding here or in Madeira?'

'In Madeira,' Rosalind told her. 'Luckily the house is big so we can put up a number of guests.'

'Myself included, I hope?' Vivienne joked.

'Of course,' Rosalind smiled.

Vivienne seemed so very much warmer than when they had first met that Rosalind began to hope that they might be friends after all.

'What are you doing for lunch on Friday?' Vivienne said with a change of topic. 'The reason I ask is that I'm driving up to London in the morning. It would be super if we could meet and have a gossip.'

'I'd like that too.'

'I've got some shopping to do at Dickens and Jones, so shall we have lunch there, say, one o'clock?'

'Let's make it half-past,' Rosalind answered, 'I've got an appointment at Moorfield's at eleven forty-five Friday morning and I'm not sure how long the specialist will keep me.'

She had dropped by at the local opticians for a sight test earlier in the week and had been referred to Moorfield's. Just to be on the safe side, the optician had said. She'd had no idea that he suspected that her blurred vision, of which she was only aware when the light was very bright, was a symptom of a rare form of hereditary blindness. The shattering news came as a bolt from the blue.

She walked out of the hospital still in a state of shock. The summer sky was faintly streaked with clouds. Pedestrians hurried along while the traffic roared by, the London buses a flash of red. She was part of the general bustle, just as she had been when she'd arrived at the hospital. The difference was that her whole world had collapsed.

She bit her lip to stop it trembling. In six months, perhaps even sooner than that, she would need someone to guide her along a busy street like this. The sight in her right eye was already failing. With some patients, the specialist had told her, both eyes were affected simultaneously. He had pointed out that because her left eye as yet showed no symptoms she would have more time to adjust.

Adjust! an inner voice cried in anguish. How could she adjust to the knowledge that the eye disease she was suffering from was passed on maternally, that not only was she going blind but that any child she and Kurt had could develop the same symptoms at any time.

She felt almost dizzy with a mixture of panic and despair. She couldn't accept the diagnosis! She had to be able to see! A woman passed her in a bright yellow and orange sundress. Seeing the vibrant shades reinforced the realisation that soon colour would exist only in her memory. She didn't think she could endure it. Colour was as essential to her as breathing. Her love of bright, bold hues was evident in every picture she had ever painted!

Like a frightened child she desperately wanted Kurt. If only he weren't in Toronto. She needed his strength, the bulwark of his love. He couldn't alter the consequences of the diagnosis but just to be in his arms would help ease the desolation a little. And yet how was she going to tell him that they would have to think seriously about the family they both wanted?

It wasn't until she saw Old Street station ahead of her that dully she remembered she was supposed to be meeting Vivienne for lunch. She was so dazed she'd made her way to the station automatically, her every instinct being to head for home.

At the ticket machines she hesitated. It wasn't possible to get a message to Vivienne to say she couldn't meet her as planned. After the trauma of the last hour the failure to keep a lunch date seemed trivial, yet some inner core of strength seemed to take over. She wasn't going to give up and go to pieces.

The first numbness of shock was wearing off, and as it did a gritty optimism took its place. There was no history of blindness in her family. Specialists had been known to make mistakes. The people on the crowded escalator, the colourful posters, every visual stimulus made it impossible for her to believe that eventually she would see in front of her eyes nothing but a blur of grey.

And even if the diagnosis was correct, the specialist had spoken of various drugs that sometimes helped. Perhaps the deterioration of her sight could be arrested.

From Oxford Circus she was quickly at Dickens and Jones. She walked through the various departments on her way to the lifts. The customers who were browsing at the perfume and jewellery counters, the atmosphere of quiet elegance that pervaded the whole store, were curiously reassuring. Inside Dickens and Jones it didn't seem possible that she could be going blind.

The lift took her up to the top floor. The carpeting muffled the sound of her footfall as she walked through into the foyer of the restaurant. She made up her mind that she'd see a different specialist. She wouldn't give up hope until she'd had a second opinion. She'd even cope somehow with losing her sight if she could just be told she and Kurt stood every chance of having a child who wasn't at risk of going blind.

'Rosalind?'

The friendly male voice startled her. She glanced up to see Andrew.

'I thought you were going to walk right past me!' he said. For a moment she continued to stare at him blankly. His gaze narrowed on her. 'Rosalind, are you OK?' he asked in concern.

'I... I'm fine,' she lied. Pulling herself together, she contrived a smile. 'I didn't mean to ignore you. I was miles away.'

'You're forgiven,' he smiled back. The cheerful note in his voice a shade forced, he asked, 'Are you meeting Kurt for lunch?'

'No, I'm meeting a friend. How about you?'

'My mother's exhibition opens tomorrow so both my parents have come up to London. I said I'd take them to lunch.'

'That's nice.' She marvelled that she could sound so natural when the optimism which had sustained her was fading and bleak despair was once again curling its cold fingers around her heart.

She caught sight of Vivienne, who was coming towards them, dramatic, chic and willowy in a tailored navy and white dress. Knife pleats set into the skirt fanned out as she walked, drawing attention to her slim legs. Her ash-blonde hair was drawn back from her face, emphasising the perfection of her features.

'I do hope I haven't kept you waiting,' she began as she joined Rosalind, bestowing a stunning smile on Andrew at the same time.

'I've only just arrived myself,' Rosalind said.

'Well, I'll be seeing you,' Andrew touched her arm, cutting in unobtrusively, as he said goodbye to her.

The faint colour beneath his tan indicated that he was a boy overawed by the charm and sophistication of an older woman.

'Who was that?' Vivienne asked.

Although her voice was light and casual, a calculating look flashed into her turquoise eyes for an instant as her gaze followed Andrew.

'Andrew's a friend from college,' Rosalind explained.

'He's obviously very interested in you,' Vivienne observed in the tone of an amused conspirator.

'We went out together for a time,' Rosalind answered absently.

'Did you? How long ago was that?'

Rosalind was so involved with the trauma of everything blindness was going to mean to her that she was almost unaware of Vivienne's curious interest in her former boyfriend.

'It was just before I met Kurt,' she said.

'Really?' Vivienne murmured as they walked through into the restaurant and were shown to a table near the window overlooking Regent Street.

An attentive waiter immediately came to give them menus to study. Rosalind glanced down at the *á la carte*, not the least bit hungry. The tightness in her throat alone meant that she didn't feel as if she could eat a thing.

Vivienne was relaying her order with light-voiced charm to the deferential waiter, her ash-blonde hair platinum in the sunlight. The same bright sunlight made the print on the menu blur in front of Rosalind's eyes. As it did so she suddenly couldn't fool herself any longer. The specialist's prognosis was right! She caught her breath imperceptibly as the full impact of the devastating truth hit her.

'You're taking a long time to make up your mind,' Vivienne said. 'Why not have the salmon mayonnaise? I know it's fattening but you don't need to worry about the calories. If anything you're almost too slim.'

The barbed compliment glanced off Rosalind. Scarcely aware of what she said, she was in such a state of turmoil she answered, 'Yes, all right, I'll have the salmon.'

'And to follow?' the waiter prompted.

'The roast chicken with...' she said, making an effort to get a grip on herself. But it was no use. To her dismay her voice choked to a halt and she burst into helpless tears.

For a minute Vivienne froze with appalled embarrassment. The next she was all concern. Reaching a hand across the table to take Rosalind's, she began, 'Darling, whatever's the matter?' A note almost of hope in her sympathetic voice, she asked, 'Seeing Andrew hasn't upset you, has it?'

Rosalind was unable to answer. It was as much as she could do to try to stifle the sobs, though she was almost beyond caring about the humiliation of breaking down in public, or of whether Andrew and his parents, who were seated at a nearby table, were looking in her direction.

'We'll order later,' Vivienne said to the waiter. 'Ask the wine waiter for a large brandy and I'll have a gin and tonic.'

Rosalind put a hand to her face, brushing away a tear and holding herself tight as she fought for control. She was grateful for the brandy. Its warmth as she took a sip helped steady her.

'Feeling better?' Vivienne asked.

Rosalind nodded. 'I...I'm sorry,' she said in a cramped whisper. 'I didn't mean to make a spectacle of myself.'

'Don't be silly,' Vivienne answered. 'Just tell me what's wrong.'

Rosalind swallowed hard. A husky catch in her voice, she said, 'I...I'm going blind.'

Her announcement was greeted by an incredulous silence.

'You can't mean it,' Vivienne began. Her cool, astute gaze narrowed on Rosalind as, like a lawyer intent on establishing the facts, she questioned, 'Are you saying that's what they told you at Moorfield's this morning? But surely something can be done? You can't mean it's incurable.'

'It's not only incurable,' Rosalind answered in despair, 'it's hereditary.' Tears brimmed in her eyes again as she said desperately, 'I don't know what to do. I can't bear the thought of not having children, of disappointing Kurt. We've already talked about a family and not waiting too long...'

'Yes, I can believe that!' Vivienne murmured as emotion snatched the end of Rosalind's sentence away. Calmly she stated as she took a sip of her gin and tonic, 'Kurt wants a son very badly. In fact, that's the only reason he's marrying you.'

Rosalind stared at her. Bewildered and shaken by one devastating shock, she couldn't seem to assimilate another.

'What did you say?' she faltered.

Well-contrived contrition showed in Vivienne's turquoise eyes.

'Oh, heavens, I'm sorry,' she exclaimed. 'I didn't mean to be so blunt. But you have to know the truth. The reason Kurt's marrying you is because he wants a son.'

'That's not true!' Rosalind protested like a flash. 'Kurt loves me!'

'For your sake I wish he did.' Anger edged Vivienne's well-modulated voice as she stated, 'I'm so furious with Kurt for this! I warned him not to hurt you and now you're going to be hurt anyway.'

'I don't know what you're talking about!'

'No, you wouldn't,' Vivienne answered, sighing. 'You're so young and trusting. You think love's all sweetness and light. You don't know how destructive it can be, any more than you really know Kurt.'

'I know that I love him and he loves me!'

'Your loyalty is touching. It also makes this all the harder for me.' Vivienne's gaze was full of appeal. 'Rosalind, you must believe me. I'm only trying to help you, to warn you.'

'Warn me of what?'

'I can see it's no use. I'm going to have to start from the beginning,' Vivienne murmured. 'I suppose Kurt told you we were at university together?'

'Yes,' Rosalind answered. 'What of it?'

In spite of her attempt to remain calm, to believe not one word the other woman said if it was against Kurt, she found she was clenching her fingers in suspense.

'It was love at first sight for both of us,' Vivienne said, a faraway look in her eyes. 'I'd never met anyone so tough and keen and amusing. There was almost a kind of telepathy between us, our minds were so closely attuned. And then of course there was the physical attraction. I know I don't have to tell you how fantastic Kurt is in bed...' A flash of triumph flickered across her face as she noted Rosalind's gaze falter. With the information she wanted, she went on, hesitant and, apparently, confused, 'You don't mean...? I assumed automatically you and Kurt were sleeping together.'

'I wanted to wait till after we were married,' Rosalind said, hating the other woman for her implication that her passionate love-affair with Kurt made her own seem tepid by comparison and doing her utmost to hide the jealousy that was clawing at her...

'Of course,' Vivienne said quickly. Her lips curved into an apologetic smile. 'I shouldn't have jumped to conclusions. Anyway, all I meant was that Kurt and I had a wonderful relationship.'

'If it was so wonderful, why did you marry Bradley?' Rosalind demanded.

'Because at that time Kurt didn't want to be tied down,' Vivienne answered. She pressed her knuckles to her lips as if bravely fighting tears. Huskily she went on, 'This is as hard for me to talk about as it must for you to hear. I...I've tried hard to be a good wife to Bradley. Even though what was between me and Kurt never stopped smouldering, I never gave him one word or one look to suggest I still felt anything for him. But then, two months ago, Bradley was away on business. Kurt rang me and asked if I'd have dinner with him. I suppose I should have said no, but he's always behaved impeccably and... and I thought I was strong enough to fight the sexual attraction between us.'

She came to an eloquent halt. All trace of colour had fled from Rosalind's face. Shaken but still fierce, she whispered, 'I don't believe you!'

'Do you think this is something I'd make up?' Vivienne asked with an anguished little laugh. 'Bradley would kill me if he knew I'd been unfaithful to him. And if he knew Kurt had asked me to leave him...!' She broke off and drew a trembling breath before going on more calmly, 'And that's what I should have done—grabbed my chance of happiness with Kurt—only the ideals I was brought up with, of honour and duty, went too deep. I turned Kurt down. He was furious, of course. The next thing I heard was that he'd got engaged to you. I knew the reason, of course. He was tired of waiting for me, and maybe, too, there was an element of revenge in it, because I'd refused to leave Bradley for him.'

Tears burned Rosalind's eyes. So many emotions were surging inside her that she felt dizzy, off balance. She didn't want to believe what Vivienne had said. Yet what motive could she have for lying?

Cold with uncertainty, she thought of how Kurt's proposal had taken her by surprise. He'd wasted no time either in asking her how she felt about children. Had he chosen her because he wasn't prepared to go on angling for Vivienne any longer?

'I...I don't believe you,' she said again, but this time her voice was choked and uncertain.

A commiserating hand was laid on her arm.

'Damn Kurt!' Vivienne murmured in a passionate undertone. 'I told him not to drag you into our private battle. It wouldn't have mattered so much if you hadn't got this terrible eye disease. Kurt would have gone ahead and married you. He might even have forgotten about me in time and you'd have been happy, that is if one ever can be happy married to a man who's in love with someone else. But he wants a son. He's told you so, hasn't he?'

Rosalind took a swift sobbing breath. The evidence was rapidly becoming an indictment. In an agony of rebellion and angry hurt she threw off Vivienne's hand. However kindly meant, she didn't want Vivienne's sympathy, not if she was the woman Kurt loved.

'When he comes back from Toronto tomorrow, would you like me to break it to him that because you're going blind you don't feel it's fair to have children?' Vivienne asked gently.

Pain tore at Rosalind's heart and a curious glint of satisfaction came into the turquoise eyes that regarded her.

'I don't care what you tell him,' she sobbed as she pushed back her chair.

In tears she hurried from the restaurant. She was almost at the lifts when Andrew caught hold of her by the arm.

'Let go of me!' she cried as he spun her round to face him.

'Rosalind, what's wrong?' he demanded.

'Nothing!' she sobbed.

'Don't give me nothing...' he began, and then broke off as she pulled away from him.

He hesitated, glancing in the direction of the restaurant where he had left his parents, before, his mouth tightening with resolve, his gaze returned to Rosalind. But it was too late. She had already disappeared through the swing doors that led to the stairs.

She ran down the several flights. Had she not been told she was going blind she might have been able to dismiss what Vivienne had said, to hold stubbornly to her belief that Kurt loved her. But, vulnerable and shaken and desperately in need of reassurance as she was, what Vivienne was claiming seemed all too possible.

She was far from sure that Kurt would have told her Vivienne had been his girlfriend at Cambridge had she not probed. It counted against him, as did the alacrity with which he'd arranged for her to meet the Lloyds. Had he hoped to hurt Vivienne by introducing her to his fiancée? Was she caught up in their private battle as Vivienne said?

She tried to remind herself of the tender hunger of his mouth when he kissed her, the desire that smouldered in the depths of his blue eyes. But had he ever actually told her he loved her? She went cold as the realisation struck her that never once had she heard him say the words.

She knew the number of his hotel and back at her flat she found herself staring at the phone in an agony of indecision. If she called him, what would she say? How could she even begin to voice her fears, to confront him with what Vivienne had said, over the phone? It had to wait till he returned.

She hardly slept at all that night. The ceiling shimmered as she stared up at it with tear-misted eyes. How was she ever going to adjust to being blind, she who was so independent and whose passion for art had been the cornerstone of her life for as long as she could remember? The answer made her heart begin to race with a mixture of panic and wretchedness. She could only face the future if she had Kurt's love to sustain her. In the depths of her misery he was the one person she wanted and she was no longer sure of him.

When Andrew called round the following afternoon to find out why she'd run from the restaurant in tears the previous day, she found she was glad of the company. She made him welcome and offered him coffee, but she refused to tell him what was wrong.

She couldn't stand the thought of seeing the shock and pity in his face when she repeated what the specialist had told her. She felt as if she was walking an emotional tightrope and any show of kindness would only cause her to burst into tears, sapping her strength, the strength she was going to need when she faced Kurt.

She was saying goodbye to Andrew at the door when Kurt's Lotus drew up at the kerb. His jeans pulled tight across his aggressive thighs, he strode up as Andrew hurried away, passing him with a nervous smile which he ignored.

Rosalind saw that his face was grimly set and his blue eyes held the glitter of steel.

'Tell me it isn't true,' he began raspingly as he seized hold of her by the elbow and pulled her towards him, uncaring that his grip bruised her.

In that single instant she knew his love had been a chimera, a false hope in her shattered world. Fate had betrayed her and now he was about to do the same. Ashen-faced, she said, the words torn from her, 'You've spoken to Vivienne, haven't you?'

'I could wring your neck for this,' he said savagely.

The force of his tightly controlled fury would have frightened her had she not been in the grip of emotions equally tumultuous herself.

'I thought you loved me enough for it to make no difference!' she hissed.

'You bloody little liar!' he exploded, his face tight and ruthless, his mouth a hard angry line. 'You didn't even have the courage to tell me yourself. You left it to Vivienne.'

'The irony is, I didn't believe her when she said this would be your reaction,' Rosalind blazed in a storm of pain. 'I suppose you want your ring back.' She snatched the solitaire diamond from her finger as she spoke. 'Well, you can have it back! I wouldn't marry you now if you begged me to. I hate you!'

Something indecipherable flickered over his rugged masculine face.

'Keep it,' he said shortly. 'Think of it as a present, not a pledge.'

'I don't want any present from you,' she replied, her eyes full of the sparks of anger and pain. He had destroyed her and, in a futile attempt to hurt him back, to make it look as if she'd never been as committed to their relationship as he'd thought, she said, 'Andrew wouldn't like me to have it.'

The tight line of Kurt's jaw clenched till the bone showed white.

'So it makes no difference to Andrew,' he said grimly. 'Well, it's lucky he's young. He doesn't know what he's taking on.'

At that her hand went up to vent all her feelings of hurt anguish and betrayal in a slap that seemed to rock him for an instant as it caught him by surprise full across one leanly muscled cheek. Horrified and afraid of what she'd done, since Kurt wasn't a man to tolerate such a blow without retaliating, Rosalind took a step backwards as the marks left by her fingers turned from white to angry red.

She gave a gasp as he snatched hold of her, cold rage leaping in his glittering eyes. But the retaliation came in a form she had not expected. His left arm went strongly round her while with his right hand he grabbed hold of her burnished hair, jerking her head back to receive his savage kiss. Held as ruthlessly as if she were in a vice, she was helpless against the brutal onslaught of his mouth, which even in its hurt held a shocking passion.

It was the last time he kissed her.

'Are you sure you did the right thing breaking off your engagement?' Manuel asked.

Lost in the byways of the past, Rosalind took an instant to focus on his question.

'I did the only thing,' she said quietly.

'Because you didn't feel you could take the risk of having a child.' Rosalind wasn't certain from his inflexion whether he expected an answer or not. In view of the real cause of her broken engagement, she was glad Manuel went on without waiting for her reply, 'Not all men want a family.'

Following his train of thought, she said, 'I know that, but I've no wish to get married, not to Kurt, not to anyone. I'm happy as I am.'

Manuel studied the stubborn tilt to her chin.

'Are you telling me you've stopped loving him?' he asked.

She nodded. 'More than that,' she said with spirit. 'I think it may be just as well he's come here. It may help me to put the past behind me.' Her voice, that was very convinced-sounding, hid the fact that she could make no sense of the tingling in the air whenever she and Kurt were together. An ever greater mystery was the anger that emanated from him, an anger that was wholly responsible, she told herself, for the sparks of confrontation he'd succeeded in striking off her. She continued, 'When he returns to London next week I'm going to put him out of my mind.'

'Completely and forever?' Manuel asked.

'Completely and forever,' she assured him.

He didn't contest her statement, but she had the feeling he wasn't entirely convinced and, maddening though it was, she found herself analysing her feelings in the light of his scepticism.

She told herself she'd meant every word of what she'd said. She wasn't in love with Kurt any more, but there was no denying that he aroused strong emotions in her. Was it because of the past, because of her shattering betrayal, or was it...? She refused to complete the thought. If she had to bludgeon her feelings into control from now until Kurt flew back to London, she wasn't going to admit that the old attraction was still there.

CHAPTER FIVE

They had sat over the meal a long time and it was late when they arrived back at the *quinta*. Collecting her clutch-bag from the dashboard, Rosalind asked, 'Would you like to come in for a nightcap?'

Manuel glanced at his watch.

'If I hadn't got to be at the office early tomorrow I'd take you up on the offer. But, since I have, I'll take a raincheck, as the Americans say.'

He saw her to the front door and, taking her key from her, inserted it into the lock. 'There you are,' he said.

'Thank you,' She gave him a smile as she said genuinely, 'It's been a lovely evening.'

'Then promise me you'll come without my having to bully you into it next time,' he joked.

'I promise,' she laughed, reaching up to kiss him lightly on the cheek.

She went inside the house and listened for a moment as his car pulled away, counting herself very lucky to have him as a friend. Then she crossed the hall and replaced her cane in the stand.

She was about to go upstairs when footsteps close at hand made her pivot sharply. They were curiously quiet, like those of a stalking Comanche, and they instilled in her the same sense of danger.

'Who's that? Who's there?' she demanded, her slightly breathless voice betraying that her sixth sense had already supplied her with the answer.

'It's me, Kurt,' came the drawling reply.

From the direction of his husky voice he was standing in the doorway to the drawing-room, leaning casually against the frame, tall, relaxed and urbane, if her intuition was correct.

'You must have had a good evening,' he observed. 'You're very late.'

'I've had a very good evening,' she replied, answering calmly but only with an effort. The aura of intimacy the warm night created made her pulse flutter nervously. Driving home with Manuel she had found the velvety stillness peaceful, but alone with Kurt, while the rest of the house was asleep, the atmosphere seemed subtly charged, unpredictable, dangerous. 'Now I'm tired and I'm going to bed.'

'Running for cover?' Kurt mocked.

'The wish being father to the thought?' she parried skilfully, giving nothing away.

'Not at all,' he returned. 'I'm simply trying to work out why you're being so wary with me.'

'How do you want me to behave?'

'How about like the woman I knew two years ago?'

There was enough meaning in his sensual remark for her skin suddenly to feel hot. She might not have slept with Kurt, but their intimate moments had been filled with pleasure and promise. It was a struggle to keep carelessness in her voice, but she managed to say with cool challenge as though she'd failed to catch any hidden innuendo, 'I thought you said I hadn't changed.'

'Well, you have,' Kurt told her. 'When we first met two years ago you were impulsive and spontaneous.'

'I was also trusting and naïve,' she retorted.

'The implication being that you were taken advantage of?' Kurt questioned sarcastically.

'It's not an implication. It's a statement of fact,' she answered. 'But I've grown up since you knew me two years ago. And these days I think twice before getting involved with anyone.'

Despite her apparent coolness her heart was beating more quickly, a fight-flight response to Kurt who had advanced almost soundlessly towards her, and now stood in front of her, threateningly male and abrasive.

'That's a little hard to credit when you're involved with Manuel,' Kurt said.

'I happen to enjoy his company.'

'He's a lot older than you are,' Kurt remarked.

'He's also utterly dependable,' she said.

Like her other verbal arrows to date, her oblique remark glanced off him. Completely unscathed, he answered, 'Which presumably is more than Andrew was.'

'You can leave Andrew out of this,' she stated.

'Is he out of it?' Kurt asked.

'Is he out of what?'

'Is he out of the picture?' Giving her no chance to claim a second time that she didn't know what he meant, he spelt it out very clearly. 'Is he a yesterday's man, a permanent back number?'

'Ought I to take your interest as a compliment?' she asked with calm irony.

'You can do if you like,' he answered. His tone said that if she was flattered she had no reason to be. 'And that's yet another question you've dodged without giving me an answer,' he pointed out.

She sensed that he was not going to give up until he got one and, defeated by his steely determination, she said coldly, 'I haven't seen Andrew or heard from him since I came home to Madeira.'

There was a short silence. Intuition told her Kurt's impassive gaze had narrowed on her.

'How much simpler,' he gibed at last, 'if you'd admitted that at the start instead of all that hedging.'

She could feel her temper deserting her. The atmosphere was too full of awareness for her peace of mind, the quietness of the night emphasising by contrast the tension that vibrated the air.

'I don't think I'm under any obligation to admit anything to you,' she answered.

'I can believe that,' he said derisively, 'which is why, now that I've got you cornered, so to speak, I intend getting some answers from you as to the state of play.'

She wasn't at all sure what was in his mind. Unable to see his face, he stood in her imagination, menacingly male, and arrogant, and still angry with her for something for which she was not to blame.

'You haven't got me cornered,' she said, while her pulse began to race.

'No?' he said.

'No,' she insisted, and then realised as she went to move that his hand was against the wall so that his arm barred her path. She felt his warm breath stir her fringe. His closeness and the clean male aroma of his aftershave made her senses quicken. Alarmed that his threatening attractiveness could have such an effect on her, she demanded, her voice far from steady, 'Get out of my way!'

'I can't believe you're frightened of me, so why this tremulous reaction because I've moved a little closer?' he taunted.

'Well, I am frightened!' Rosalind declared, clenching her hands to stop them from shaking. 'I know that hard note in your voice! You're angry with me and you've got me pinned against the wall. I haven't forgotten the brutal way you kissed me the last time. And I can't even defend myself because I'm blind.'

She sensed him stiffen. The next instant she was free.

'I wasn't about to be brutal,' he said, his tone suggesting that he did not appreciate the low opinion she had of him. 'It hadn't occurred to me that I was scaring you.'

Immeasurably relieved that he had given her more space, she felt the tension drain from her shoulders. Her tone cool and measured, she said as she recovered her poise, 'That's because you have no conception of what it's like to be blind.'

'No. I suppose I don't,' he agreed.

'You sound almost sympathetic!' she said, both surprised and angered by his inflexion. Kurt was as hard as granite, so why had he given such a humane answer? Like the gentleness in his touch when he had guided her and retrieved her cane, it was a mystery that prompted her to say, 'It's no wonder I find you impossible to understand!'

'If you find me hard to understand, believe me, it's mutual.'

'Exactly what's hard to understand about me?' she challenged.

'Rather than make a list, let's tackle it one point at a time,' he said, sarcasm in his voice. 'The first one being Manuel. What's your relationship with him? You tell me he's your boyfriend. Julia says he's only a friend.'

'Julia, as you well know, is matchmaking,' Rosalind answered.

'It's one extreme to the other with you, isn't it?' Kurt remarked with amused contempt. 'First you pick up with a boy. Now it seems you're looking for a father-figure.'

She drew a deep breath, trying to calm her simmering anger. Why couldn't Kurt leave her alone instead of determinedly forcing a confrontation? Meaning to bring the conversation to a frosty conclusion and then to make her escape, she said, 'What I'm looking for is my affair.'

'Is Manual your lover?'

The blunt question took her unawares and as a reflex response she launched into a counter-attack.

'Why should you care one way or the other? Or was Manuel right when he suggested you were jealous of him?'

There was a short pause. Her senses told her Kurt was studying her closely, perhaps with a malevolent glint in his blue eyes as finally he succeeded in getting a rise out of her.

'So Manuel thinks I'm jealous.' She visualised the mocking smile that played at the corners of his sensual mouth as he asked, 'And what's your opinion?'

His voice was silky, sending a prickle of alarm over her skin. The late-hour inquisition she was being subjected to meant that she had strong grounds for answering tauntingly that she believed he was jealous. But some instinct warned her not to add to the tension that was vibrating in the air. Backing down, she answered, 'I...I haven't the least idea.'

'But just the same, you're wondering if the reason I'm up so late was to check what time you came in.'

'Don't be ridiculous!' she retorted, the warmth in her cheeks betraying that he had read her thoughts.

'Let me set the record straight.' His tone was just as silky as before, yet held a paradoxically abrasive note. She caught her breath as his thumb grazed her cheek in a little caress. 'The reason I got out of bed and came downstairs was to do you a service.'

Her thoughts blazed. She had supposed he was immaculately dressed in a dinner-jacket from his evening at Reid's. Now, as a result of his words, a different yet more devastatingly male image flashed into her mind, an image of him bronzed and naked beneath his robe.

She should have realised from his almost soundless tread when he had approached her that he was barefoot, just as his body heat should have told her he was wearing the minimum of clothing. Her heart was beating erratically in response to his negligent caress and, unable to credit his insolent implication, she said in a voice that shook with temper, 'I beg your pardon!'

His laughter, deep, amused and very masculine, mocked her.

'Such outrage and such vanity!' he gibed. 'It seems you've misunderstood me, Rosalind. I didn't mean I got out of bed to give you sexual satisfaction. I meant——'

He broke off as in a blaze of temper she tried to push past him. But instead of allowing her to pass he caught hold of her wrist, holding her his helpless prisoner.

'Let go of me!' she stormed.

'Well, surprise, surprise!' he taunted, an edge of satisfaction in his voice. 'So you do still have a temper.'

'You're despicable,' she hissed. 'How dare you insult me with your innuendoes?'

'No,' Kurt corrected her as he fired back with his answer. 'You chose to interpret what I was saying as a sexual innuendo. It says quite a lot about the degree of frustration in your life.'

Angry colour stained her cheeks, enhancing the lovely lines of her face.

'The frustration in my life is due to the fact that I'm blind,' she flashed. 'Not...'

'Go on,' he prompted as she trailed off.

'Not because...' Finding the sentence impossible to complete, she rephrased it. 'Not everyone finds celibacy frustrating!'

'Are you telling me your relationship with Manuel is platonic?' Kurt said, incredulity in his husky voice.

Angrily she realised that temper had tripped her into making an admission she most certainly wouldn't have made otherwise.

'You're insufferable!' she snapped with hatred.

'And you, at last, are acting more like the fiery redhead I'd remembered,' Kurt replied. 'I was beginning to think she'd been replaced by a marble statue.'

It infuriated Rosalind that he should have succeeded in what had obviously been his intention all along. Why had she let him needle her into losing her calm? She drew breath for a crushing reply and then, hearing a faint miaow, she checked what she'd been about to say. Her Siamese communicated with a variety of little cries and she had no difficulty in interpreting this tiny mew as plaintive. Distracted by it, she asked, 'Where's Cleo?'

'Cleo's just used up one of her nine lives. The adventures of your cat explain why I'm up this late.'

'I... I don't understand. What adventures? Is Cleo hurt?' Rosalind asked, concern taking over from her anger.

'No, she's fine,' Kurt told her before explaining, 'I'd dozed off when I was woken by what sounded like a baby crying. For an instant I thought perhaps it accounted for the defensive way you've been acting with me.'

Having made an utter fool of herself with him once by jumping to the wrong conclusion, she wasn't inclined to do the same again. Wanting to make sure of her facts, she began, 'I'm not sure what you're saying.'

'No?' he said cynically.

'No!' she retorted, stung. 'But if you're suggesting——'

'I'm not,' he cut in, an abrasive edge to his voice. 'After all, why would you have lied to me?'

'I haven't got a clue what you're talking about!'

'Is that an oblique way of telling me to leave the subject alone?' he sneered.

By now she was completely adrift in bewilderment.

'What subject?' she demanded.

'I'm talking about the reason you and I broke up,' he said. His inflexion sardonic, he asked, 'Does that jog your memory?'

She felt a sharp twist of pain, but having lost her temper she wasn't going to cap it by bursting into tears. Every time he referred to her blindness the harshness in his tone seemed to imply that the affliction was somehow her fault. It was an effort to answer him at all, let alone calmly, but when at last she did there was scarcely a trace of a catch in her voice.

'I remember everything,' she said.

'And what exactly am I supposed to make of that enigmatic remark?' he demanded.

'Nothing,' she told him, conscious that the tension in the air seemed once again to be gathering ominously. Her chin tilted a little as she added, anticipating the interpretation he would automatically put on her reply, 'And I'm not being hostile or defensive. Why should I be, since you don't mean a thing to me any longer?'

'That's an interesting question,' he observed.

'Is it? Why?'

'You know there's nothing I find more infuriating than that calm but mutinous act you keep putting on for me.'

'What makes you think it's an act?' she asked.

The moment the words were out she regretted them. Kurt's dangerously mild tone should have counselled her against another answer in the same vein.

'Is it your intention to provoke me?'

'No, of course not,' she denied, her heart thumping. 'You were the one who started this conversation.'

As she was speaking she heard the silvery tinkle of the little bell Cleo wore on her collar and the next instant there was a nudge at her ankle. Quickly she picked the little cat up and then exclaimed as the Siamese snuggled against her shoulder.

'Cleo, what's happened to you? You're all damp.'

'Glad of a diversion?' Kurt gibed.

Afraid that she had taxed his forbearance to the limit, she *was* very glad of a diversion. But rather than admit to the fact she asked, 'What's Cleo been up to?'

'I've just hooked her out of the water butt on the veranda,' Kurt replied. 'She must have climbed up on it and somehow fallen in.'

'Why didn't you tell me?' Rosalind said, shocked but thankful that the little cat was safe.

'If you remember, I was in the middle of telling you when you accused me of making sexual innuendos.' Kurt's voice was mocking. He scratched Cleo's head and the Siamese purred more loudly, enjoying the caress. 'It was lucky I happened to hear her desperate miaowing.'

'She could have drowned,' Rosalind murmured in consternation. If her perception was right, Kurt had stopped stroking the cat, but even so she took care not to move lest inadvertently her hand brushed his.

Her inner radar told her he was far too close while her imagination summoned up his forceful features, the strong line of his jaw, the masculine sternness of his mouth. The contempt she held him in did not make her senses immune to his rugged masculinity. Stubbornly fighting her awareness of him, she spoke to the little cat.

'You've had a narrow escape, Cleo.' To Kurt she remarked, 'I think it's frightened her, but at least her fur's starting to fluff up.'

'I was drying her off with a towel when you came in,' Kurt said. 'I suggest you get the lid of the water butt repaired, just in case Cleo goes clambering on it again.'

'I will,' Rosalind said. 'I'll speak to João about it first thing in the morning.

'Who's João?'

'Maria's husband. He sees to the garden and does any odd jobs round the place.'

Cleo suddenly sneezed and struggled to be put down. Rosalind dropped the Siamese on to her chocolate-coloured paws.

'I...I'm very grateful to you, Kurt,' she said. Feeling that she had expressed her appreciation quite adequately, and not inclined to linger talking any longer when the atmosphere was so full of undercurrents, she added stiltedly, 'I'll see you in the morning.'

'Relax, Rosalind.' He sounded amused by her coolness. 'I'm not about to extract payment from you in kind.'

'I didn't think you were!'

'Didn't you?' he drawled. 'If the comments you've made tonight are anything to go by, you seem very much to have the idea that I intend kissing you.'

'That's not true!' she said, and hoped that the light was dim enough for him not to see that she was blushing.

Kurt didn't contest her statement. Instead, on the same tack, he stated, 'I take it Manuel kissed you goodnight.'

As it happened *she* had kissed *him*, but, too intent on parrying Kurt's remarks to split hairs and conscious all the time of the menacing sexual chemistry that pulsed between them, she demanded, 'So what if he did? He's a friend.'

'We've agreed to be friends, too.'

Her heart skipped a beat as she realised suddenly what Kurt was driving at. Holding her ground by a sheer effort of will, she said coldly, 'If you're referring to our conversation earlier, you were the one who seemed to think we could be friends.'

'Panicking at the thought of a kiss, Rosalind?' Kurt's husky voice was mocking.

'Not in the least,' she lied. She was trembling and she wanted nothing more than to flee to her room, but she couldn't afford to let Kurt make the surmises that would surely follow his taunting question if she didn't challenge it. Just as importantly, she needed to convince herself. She went on, 'It doesn't throw me into a panic because the fire went out of our relationship two years ago. You can't breathe life back into cold ashes. Now, goodnight.'

Her parting line delivered, she took a step towards the stairs and then gave a little gasp as Kurt caught hold of her by the arm. He jerked her back towards him. She collided with his chest, the contact with his lean man's body momentarily robbing her of breath. Immediately his arms went round her, wrapping her tightly to him as he bent his head.

Far from resisting, she found herself meeting his kiss exactly as if she had been expecting it. Everything, from their low-key sparring to his sarcasm and her flashes of temper, had served to make it the inevitable conclusion to the warm, sultry night.

She hated Kurt, yet in the madness of the moment her mouth parted under his, a river of forgotten sensations running hotly through her veins. She didn't care that the arms that held her were like iron bands or that his lips almost bruised hers in the instant before he switched the kiss to one of sensual demand.

As though the hunger of his mouth was appeasing an eternity of need for both of them, she stayed in his embrace, her senses reeling and her body feverish as she kissed him back. Her fingers threaded into his hair as his hands caressed the slim plane of her back. It seemed she had waited forever to be kissed again like this, demandingly, possessively, so that thoughts and senses merged into a blaze of passion. And then she pulled free, breathing hard, her heart hammering.

For an instant neither of them spoke. She sensed Kurt's blue, rapier-keen gaze on her. The rise and fall of his deep chest told her that his breathing was as altered as her own. Shaken by the maelstrom of desire she had felt in his arms, she was flushed and incapable of uttering a sound.

'It seems you were wrong,' Kurt said quietly. 'The ashes of our relationship aren't cold and lifeless, not by a long shot.'

CHAPTER SIX

ALONE in her room, Rosalind leaned back against the door, her heart racing. Unconsciously her fingers moved to her lips which only moments before had been covered by Kurt's. Just to think of his kiss was to recall the feel of his mouth on hers, the wild, feverish sensations he had aroused in her.

She should never have let it happen. Yet how could she have prevented it? Kurt had been too swift for her, too much in control of the situation. It was almost as though he had planned it, a ridiculous suspicion when he wouldn't have been downstairs at all had her Siamese not needed rescuing.

Why had he kissed her? she wondered, as she advanced into the room. Had it been some kind of experiment to see if she would respond to him again? Or had he simply been curious to find out if she still meant anything to him?

She winced as she banged her knee. Her mind was so full of racing thoughts that she had forgotten to count her steps from the door. Stretching out her hand, she identified the piece of furniture she had walked into as her dressing-table.

She sat down at it, fumbled with the chain around her neck and took off her bracelets. She should never have lingered at the foot of the stairs, matching words with Kurt. She should have bolted, not tried to prove something to herself.

She knew that, had she been able to see, her reflection in the mirror would have shown that her cheeks were flushed and that there were sparks of gold in the depths of her brown eyes. Kurt had likened her to a marble statue and that was how she had felt. But now the statue had turned into a passionate, living woman again.

An inner voice spoke sharply in rebuke. It was one kiss, that was all—and what did it mean?

'Nothing,' she muttered.

She hadn't been so calm and detached only to allow Kurt to shatter the wall she had built around her emotions. Yet, as she lay in bed, deep inside was the knowledge that her defences were already in ruins.

The warm breeze that stirred the curtains at the window seemed sensual as it fanned her skin. The erotic mastery with which Kurt had captured her in his embrace refused to be put out of mind. She had wanted him to kiss her. She still wanted him, and the knowledge was startling, shattering.

Wakeful and hot, she threw back the covers. She hadn't forgotten the sweet excitement of desire, but always until now she had managed to thrust the memories of those feelings aside in ruthless dedication to her work. In a determined attempt not to think of Kurt any more she turned on to her side and dragged her pillow down under her cheek. She didn't want to remember or to feel.

She concentrated on making her mind a blank, but it was no use. Every time she closed her eyes it was to see Kurt's rugged face, to remember everything he had once meant to her.

When she had first lost her sight the nights had seemed endless. The tremendous emotional stress of being newly blind had meant she'd been too tense to sleep. Now once again she lay staring wakefully up at the ceiling. In an attempt to unwind, she turned the radio on quietly. But it didn't stop her from replaying all the events of the past, over and over in her thoughts. Nothing could do that.

She did drift off eventually for a few hours, but woke, conscious that her sleep had been shallow. Hazy sexual images lingered in her mind. The desires she had hoped to forget in the oblivion of sleep had surfaced instead in confused forbidden dreams.

She swung her legs out of bed and, drawing on her wrap, walked over to the open window to lean on the sill. The stillness that was broken only by the birdsong and the hiss of the sprinklers on the lawns told her that it was very early.

I was just beginning to get my life back together, she thought. Why did Kurt have to come to Madeira? I should have been safe here!

Knowing that she wouldn't sleep again and needing to be occupied, she showered, dressed and went downstairs. In her studio she removed the thin plastic cover from the sculpture she was working on.

Her fingers explored the firm clay. The underlying shapes and sculptures were already established. A chubby baby boy sat on his mother's lap, her beads clasped in one tiny fist. The modelling of the figures she had deliberately left sketchy, wanting to draw attentoin to the look of love and tenderness on the mother's face.

Taking a modelling tool, she hollowed out the eye sockets. Then the implement was laid aside. In general she used few tools, preferring to rely on her fingers. Working directly with her hands seemed to create a rapport between the clay and herself. It was as if the life in her fingers imparted character to the damp clay.

She'd told Manuel that when she was at work in her studio she was so absorbed she forgot everything else. That had been true in the past, but this morning her thoughts kept wandering to Kurt. She tried to persuade herself that there would be no repetition of what had happened between them last night. Kurt was heartless and he'd wanted to test her emotions. There was no reason for him to repeat the experiment.

Except in her heart she knew there had been more to it than that. His kiss hadn't been gentle, yet even in its angry passion it had held a vast and deliberate expertise. It had been as if he had wanted not so much to master her as to make her respond to him with sweet abandon.

Just what cruel game was he playing? she asked herself. But no answer sprang to mind as, pinching the clay, she formed the mother's cheekbones before sculpting the tender line of the mouth.

She remembered Kurt's skill at chess. She'd been a good player herself before she'd lost her sight, but she'd only ever beaten him once and it had taken every ounce of her concentration. Just as then she'd never been certain of how he would attack, so now she had no idea what his next move would be. She only knew that she felt frighteningly vulnerable.

Outside, the sky had turned a brilliant blue. Critically she assessed her work, and then, satisfied with it, she shrugged her shoulders, easing the slight stiffness that came from bending close for so long over her sculpture. She wasn't wearing her braille watch but her inner clock told her it must be time at last for breakfast.

She was crossing the hall when she heard the sound of footsteps and a familiar male voice said from behind her, 'Good morning.'

A tinge of colour came into her face. The next instant she had her emotions tightly battened down, her semblance of composure perfect as she pivoted towards the speaker.

'Good morning, Kurt. I hope you slept well?'

'Fine, thanks.' The inflexion of his voice mocked her cool enquiry that was so much at variance with the passion with which she had kissed him the previous night. 'Did you?'

'Like a log,' she lied. As if to give weight to her answer she added, 'I always do.'

'Obviously you have a clear conscience.'

'What does that mean?'

'People who have a clear conscience are supposed to sleep well.'

'Why shouldn't I have a clear conscience?' she challenged.

'You're very prickly this morning,' he observed.

On the defensive, it was hard for her to be anything else. Not even the loss of her most important sense seemed able to blunt her awareness of him. With her central vision destroyed she couldn't even make him out as an indistinct shadow against the perpetual mist of grey, yet in every nerve she seemed conscious of his tall, virile frame. His chiselled features were etched indelibly in her memory. His husky, slightly abrasive voice was another reminder of his powerful male charisma.

'It's just that I'm tired of being sniped at,' she said.

'What makes you think I'm sniping at you?' There was a touch of impatience in Kurt's question.

'I can't see your expression. I have to gauge from your tone whether you're being sarcastic or not. Perhaps I've got it wrong, in which case I'm sorry, but it doesn't sound to me as if you're making innocuous friendly conversation!'

'Was that how you expected me to be, friendly and innocuous?' he asked cuttingly.

'When are you going to stop blaming me?' The words were torn from her. 'I couldn't help...' The catch in her voice forced her to break off.

His tone a shade clipped, Kurt said, 'Look, let's call a cease-fire, shall we?'

'If you think we can,' she murmured, struggling to regain her poise.

'It would help if you'd at least meet me halfway,' he pointed out.

It would also help if her feelings for him were as dead as she kept claiming they were!

'I'm doing my best,' she said, the set of her mouth defiant. Switching from the defensive to an oblique attack, she went on, 'But if you want a ceasefire you'll match your actions to your words.'

'Which action specifically are you referring to?' he said.

The touch of sarcasm in his voice was all it took in her current mood to make her spark, 'I think you know! But if you want me to spell it out, I object to being grabbed hold of and kissed against my will.'

'Against your will? When did I kiss you against your will?'

'Last night!'

'I didn't notice you putting up much of a struggle,' he pointed out.

It was her turn to be sarcastic. 'And I suppose if I had you'd have let me go straight away!'

'We'll try it out some time if you'd like,' he offered, amusement in his husky voice.

'I wouldn't like!' she snapped.

'OK, then we won't try it.'

His words seemed to be intended to placate her. She wasn't sure how she was meant to take them, since she had no way of telling if the suggestion of a sardonic smile showed on his rugged face. It was maddening to have to rely on instinct and not to know for certain whether or not a muscle twitched at the corner of his masculine mouth.

'You're being very conciliatory this morning,' she said warily.

She was sounding him out. His tone when he answered would tell her whether he was being sincere or taking a gibe at her.

'The aim, if you remember, was to establish a cease-fire,' he answered.

His husky voice was dry but it was devoid of mockery. Since jousting with him only made the warring currents in the air more unpredictable, it seemed sensible to take a calming breath and agree.

'I'm willing to give a truce a try.'

'Then let's recommence this conversation,' Kurt said, commenting, 'You must have started work early this morning.'

'How do you know?' she questioned.

'You're not the only detective.' The trace of humour in his tone recalled the joke they had shared the previous evening. 'You have a smudge of clay on your cheek.' As he spoke he brushed it away with his thumb. 'Do you always start work so early?' he asked.

'I couldn't sl...' she began, flustered by his firm but gentle touch, and then could have bitten her tongue. Hoping he hadn't noticed her unthinking slip, she went on quickly, 'I couldn't risk the clay drying out. It's important to catch it just right. When the clay is short it's hard to work with.'

'How do you mean, short?' he enquired.

'It's when the clay starts to crack and break,' she explained the term. 'When it's perfect to work with it's called silky. If I'd let it wait any longer I'd have had to mist the sculpture with water using a spray gun, but though that makes the surface pliable it's not as good as when all the clay is the perfect consistency.'

'I'd be interested to see some of your work.'

The idea of his prowling round the private territory of her studio disturbed her, though she wasn't prepared to acknowledge it.

'How about after breakfast?' she asked, hoping that he'd be too busy to take her up on the offer.

'I've already had breakfast,' he told her. 'I'm off now to have another look at Julia's building plot. Let's make it this afternoon when I've more time.'

'OK,' she agreed.

She fancied his gaze followed her as, taking her chance to escape, she went through into the dining-room. Why did she have to be so shatteringly conscious of him? she asked herself fiercely.

She was determined not to allow him to erode the attitude of frosty civility she had adopted towards him. Yet already he had succeeded in setting a spark to her temper on more than one occasion. A week wasn't long, she kept telling herself, yet it seemed an eternity when her emotions were under siege and she was uneasily aware that there was too much static in the air between them for any truce to be lasting.

She paused on the threshold to the veranda, hearing a tiny bell. Cleo, it seemed, was washing placidly in the sun, none the worse apparently for her adventures the previous night. With a short sigh Rosalind wished she were equally resilient.

The rustling of the pages of a magazine told her that Julia was sitting at the breakfast table.

'What a shame. You've only just missed Kurt,' she began, setting her magazine aside as Rosalind joined her.

'I met him in the hall.'

'Did you? What did he have to say?'

'He asked me to elope with him and said he couldn't live another day without me,' she quipped as she found her napkin and spread it on her lap.

'Rosalind, be serious,' her aunt protested.

'That's not easy when you seem set on pairing me off with him.'

'I might succeed, what's more, if you weren't so stubborn,' her aunt asserted. 'You're so like your father at times!'

Julia had felt it her duty as far as was possible to take her niece and her widowed brother under her wing after Rosalind's mother had died. Evidently it had never crossed her mind that the reason Bernard had to dig in his heels on occasion was because she was so sure she knew what was best. But, fond of her aunt, Rosalind didn't point the fact out.

'Will you start with juice this morning?' Julia continued. 'There's orange or grapefruit.'

'I'll have grapefruit juice, please.' There was the sound of the drink being poured and then the glass was placed by her hand. 'How was your evening last night?' she asked.

'It was most exciting!' came the reply.

'Exciting? Reid's?' Rosalind sounded puzzled.

'Kurt suggested we go on to the casino afterwards,' her aunt explained. 'I've never seen anyone play blackjack like it. Kurt apparently has this system based on probability. It was very complicated, and I can't say I really understood it, but it certainly works! He caused quite a stir at the tables.'

'I can imagine,' Rosalind murmured.

Devastatingly attractive and with an edge of ruthlessness in his character, Kurt must have commanded the attention of every woman present as he gambled on the cards with cool authority. Could she really blame him for not wanting a wife who was blind, a wife who couldn't share fully in his life? Had his love not been a cruel sham from the very start, perhaps she could have forgiven him.

'Then I decided I'd try my hand at roulette,' Julia went on. 'Do you know, I've never been so lucky? Every time I bet on the numbers fifteen and twenty-two they came up for me.'

'What made you choose them?' The vivacity in her aunt's voice lent the warmth of a smile to her own.

'I didn't,' Julia said. 'Kurt did, not of course that you can play roulette with a system. He must have picked the numbers at random, or perhaps they have some sort of significance for him.'

Rosalind didn't reply immediately. Was it pure coincidence that Kurt had chosen to gamble on the date of her birthday and the date on which they had got engaged? Or was the past as much in his thoughts as it was in hers?

Fool, she told herself promptly. She might be sentimental but Kurt most certainly wasn't. He was as hard as nails. She doubted he even remembered the date of her birthday, let alone that it had been the twenty-second of May when he'd asked her to marry him.

Refusing to allow him to dominate the conversation any longer, she asked, changing the topic, 'What were you reading when I came and sat down?'

'An article on interior design. It's rather soon, I know, to be thinking of colour schemes when the new house isn't even built yet, but I want an idea of what's fashionable at the moment.' The glossy pages of the magazine rustled as Julia turned to the section she wanted. 'What do you think of this? Borscht-red with white and peacock-green accents.'

'Is that what you've decided on?' Rosalind asked, keeping her opinion to herself till she was sure.

'Heavens, no!' Julia laughed.

'Good, because it sounds terrible,' Rosalind said, laughing too. 'But I didn't want to say so if you were planning to decorate the whole house in it!'

'Credit me with a little better taste than that!' Julia joked. 'No, this is what I have in mind, at least for the lounge. Walls the colour of pink quartz with periwinkle-blue draperies and accents of white and Dubonnet.'

'That could look really good,' Rosalind agreed, picturing it in her mind.

They were interrupted by the housekeeper who came on to the patio to announce, 'You're wanted on the phone, *senhorita*.'

The caller was Isobel, her father's girlfriend. In her early thirties, slim, dark-haired and attractive she ran a handicraft shop in Funchal selling a whole variety of wicker goods that the island was noted for. She asked Rosalind what her plans were for the afternoon and then said, 'Would you like to come over for lunch? I'm not going into the shop today and it would be nice to have some company and a chat.'

Rosalind hesitated. Her sculpture was nearly finished. A day's uninterrupted work and she would have it completed and fired. But she didn't want to appear unfriendly by turning down Isobel's invitation and Kurt's gibe that she'd turned into a recluse had stung a little. Deciding quickly, she said, 'I'd like that. What time shall I come?'

'Shall we say one o'clock?'

'I'll just check there's someone to drive me,' Rosalind said, and then smiled as Maria, who came into the hall at that moment, overheard and announced,

'Joõa will take you, of course.'

João's duties did not include acting as chauffeur and Rosalind didn't like to trespass on his goodwill without asking first. His wife, however, had no such compunction. If Senhorita Rosalind wished to go into Funchal then it was her husband's job to take her there.

'It's OK, João will bring me,' Rosalind relayed the information over the phone.

'Good. I'll see you later then. Oh, and bring a swimsuit. I thought we'd laze round the pool after lunch.'

João dropped her outside Isobel's house and said that he would be back to collect her at half-past three. The silver-grey Mercedes pulled away from the kerb and, with her cane tapping, Rosalind went up the steps to the front door.

She knew from the fragrance that greeted her that the town garden was ablaze with flowers. In general her other senses compensated well for her lost sight but at times she missed painfully not being able to see the bright profusion that was Funchal, the bougainvillaea that trailed over walls and roofs in intoxicating waves of scarlet and magenta.

Isobel had prepared a salad. Followed by cheesecake topped with fresh pineapple it made a light refreshing lunch. Afterwards they sat on loungers at the side of the swimming-pool, the circle of shade from a large umbrella protecting them from the full glare of the sun. The faintest slap of water against the pool's tiled sides added to the indolent atmosphere.

'What's the architect you've got staying with you like?'

Isobel's voice broke into the calm of Rosalind's daydream. Thrown by the question, she faltered, 'He...' and then admitted reluctantly, 'Actually I...I was engaged to him once.'

'I'd no idea.' There was no mistaking the inflexion of interest in the reply. 'Tell me more.'

Inwardly Rosalind despaired. It seemed impossible to put Kurt out of her thoughts. Lazing by the pool, she had actually forgotten him for an instant. Now she was reminded again.

'I knew him two years ago in London,' she said.

'And?' Isobel prompted.

'And what?'

'Is the magic still there?'

Her heart contracted with an odd twist of pain.

'No,' she spoke lightly to conceal her feelings. 'I'm afraid not.'

Isobel threw her long, dark plait over her shoulder, making a flicking sound. 'Pity.' She smiled.

'Why?'

'I was hoping to marry you off,' she joked.

'Not you too!' It was hard to laugh but somehow Rosalind managed it. 'I've already got Julia playing matchmaker for all she's worth.'

'I wonder what her motives are,' Isobel said. 'You see, with me...I... Oh, damn!' she exclaimed softly. 'I knew I was going to manage this badly.'

'Manage what?'

'No, let's forget it. Would you like some more iced tea?'

'What I'd like is for you to finish what you were saying.'

'I...I'm just so afraid you're going to take this the wrong way.'

'Does this have something to do with Dad?' Rosalind's guess was a shot in the dark.

'Yes,' came the reluctant answer. There was a pause and then Isobel went on, 'Rosalind, I love your father very much. For a long time I thought he had no intention of marrying again. I knew that if I wanted to continue our relationship that was something I had to accept. I was grateful that he chose me to be his partner at bridge, his companion at dinner or for a concert and his confidante. But this last year things have changed. We've become so much closer. If it weren't...'

She trailed off and Rosalind supplied the words, 'You're saying if it weren't for me, Dad would ask you to marry him.'

'I don't want to be unkind,' Isobel insisted. 'I like you very much and I'd hate us to quarrel.' Her voice steadied and became more determined, 'But Bernard means everything to me. He knows I'm possessive. I can't help it. I always have been. If the three of us were to live together at the *quinta* there would be bound to be tension. But if when Julia's new house is built you'd make your home with your aunt, the problem would be solved for all of us.'

'I see,' Rosalind said tightly. 'I suppose it hasn't occurred to you that if I'm a burden to my father I'd be a burden to Julia too.'

'I didn't mean it like that,' Isobel protested.

'You mean you wouldn't have put it quite so bluntly!' Rosalind retorted, and then broke off, forcing herself to be positive and reasonable. 'I can see your suggestion makes sense in a lot of ways,' she went on, 'but there's an alternative which would suit me much better. I could get a place of my own.'

'Your father would never accept that. He worries enough about you as it is.'

'I know,' Rosalind nodded. 'Because I'm blind he's very protective. I've tried to explain to him that I need to be independent and to manage on my own.'

'But you think if I added my voice to yours, together we might convince him?' Isobel said.

'Yes, I do,' Rosalind answered.

She spoke calmly, though she was very close to the end of her tether. Before Kurt had arrived, her patience had seemed limitless. Now she felt that with any more provocation her control would snap abruptly and whoever happened to be on the receiving end of her temper would be left wondering dazedly at the explosion.

'I'll talk to him about it when he comes back from New York,' Isobel said. Letting the subject drop, she asked, 'Are you going to the fiesta on Wednesday?'

Rosalind was about to answer Isobel's question when the sound of footsteps on the terrace diverted her attention. One lightly tapping set belonged without a doubt to the maid. The other, a man's, made her turn her head in the direction of the house like a deer scenting danger.

'Kurt?' she murmured. 'I'm sure that's his step.'

'Well, it certainly isn't João,' Isobel said. 'Whoever's called to collect you is tall, strong-featured and dark-haired. Is he your architect friend?'

A nod confirmed Isobel's guess. The next moment a husky masculine voice drawled, 'Hello, ladies. You've certainly chosen an ideal way to spend the afternoon.'

'Come and join us,' Isobel invited. She introduced herself. 'I'm Isobel Fonseca.'

'Kurt Wilding,' he replied. 'How do you do?'

His charisma and charm were apparent even in such a customary exchange. There was a faint creak as he sat down on one of the loungers and stretched out his long legs.

'Why have you come to meet me, and not João?' Rosalind asked.

She tried to frame the question casually, to conceal her dismay that he and not João had called to pick her up. She'd been completely unselfconscious in her coral and gold bikini, the straps of her top crossing prettily over her breasts to fasten in a bow behind her neck, while she'd been talking to Julia. But with her ex-fiancé sitting alongside her, his arm practically brushing hers, she felt far too naked for comfort.

'I had some letters to post and as I was driving into Funchal anyway I said I'd call for you.'

There was a faint edge of mockery in his voice that suggested he knew she would have preferred João as her chauffeur. It was too subtle for Isobel to catch. She asked, 'Is this your first visit to Madeira?'

'There's not a great deal of demand for architects on a small island,' Kurt joked.

'I suppose not,' Isobel laughed. 'I wondered if you'd holidayed here.'

'I'm sure I could get hooked on relaxing in the sun,' he said, a smile in his voice, 'but until now when I've taken a break I've tended to choose a very active holiday, somewhere off the beaten track. I enjoy roughing it for a change.'

'I'm intrigued,' Isobel said, responding automatically to the magnetism of his personality. 'What sort of countries have you visited?'

'Alaska, the Yukon and several in South America,' he answered. 'Last summer I spent a month trekking in Bolivia and Peru. It was tough going until everyone in the party got used to the altitude and the thin air, but after that it was a great experience. Approaching the Inca city of Machu Picchu is something I'll never forget.'

'I don't think I could keep up with you,' Isobel laughed.

Rosalind's fingers curved about the armrests of her chair. Athletic and adventurous, until she'd lost her sight she'd shared Kurt's love of the outdoors.

Now, even though she was still fit and lithe, her blindness meant she must always move tentatively lest she stumble. Even had Kurt had loved her, how she would have slowed him down had she married him!

'Can I offer you a drink?' Isobel was continuing. 'Would you like iced tea or gin and lime?'

'I'll have gin and lime.'

Isobel's footsteps retreated. In the ensuing silence Rosalind sensed Kurt's keen gaze on her.

'You've hardly said a word since I arrived,' he observed. 'What's wrong?'

The genuine note of concern in his voice caught her unawares.

'Nothing's wrong,' she bluffed.

Swinging her feet off the lounger on to the sun-warmed paving of the patio, she reached for her overshirt. She'd left it thrown over the back of her chair but her searching fingers failed to locate it immediately. Kurt handed it to her with an ironic, 'Are you finding the sun too much?'

She was finding his nearness too much, as undoubtedly he suspected. Glad to slip on her overshirt to hide her figure from his masculine gaze, she insisted, 'I don't want to get sunburned.'

'Your coolness is very beguiling but it's also become more and more of a challenge.'

The drawling remark made in his sensual husky voice sent a hot little shiver tracing over her skin.

'I thought we'd agreed to a truce,' she murmured.

'So you're putting up a white flag. Well, I'm ready to discuss terms.'

He was ribbing her gently and she found she was smiling in response. The difference was so great when he spoke to her without the jeer of sarcasm that unconsciously she dropped her guard with him.

'Magnanimous of you!' she teased.

'I'm a magnanimous sort of person. That's why I came to Madeira.'

Her heart seemed to skip a beat. How was she to construe his remark? She forced herself to be sensible. Of course he didn't mean he was now able to overlook her blindness! The rapport that was growing between them was no reason for her to go jumping to wild conclusions.

Angry with herself, she was all ready to break their cease-fire with a lightly barbed comment when footsteps heralded Isobel's return.

CHAPTER SEVEN

ICE tinkled against glass as Isobel announced, 'One gin and lime as requested.' Addressing her question to Kurt, she asked as she relaxed in her chair, 'How long will it be once the plans are drawn up before Julia's new house is completed?'

'She'd like to move in around Christmas-time, she tells me, so I'll hurry things along all I can for her.'

'I'll leave you two to chat while I get changed,' Rosalind put in, getting to her feet. 'It's all right, I won't fall in the pool,' she added, anticipating Kurt's offer to see her indoors.

'Are you as fiercely independent with everyone as you are with me?' he mocked gently.

'I don't like being reminded constantly that I'm vulnerable,' she answered.

'An interesting choice of words.'

She blushed. She certainly hadn't intended to imply any more than that she wanted to forget her disability. It was tempting to challenge his remark, but a reluctance to joust with him in front of Isobel stopped her.

In the house she slipped on the stylish wrap skirt which matched her overshirt. The full skirt emphasised the neatness of her waist, while her shirt, which she left unbuttoned to show her bikini top, gave her outfit a breezy, summery look.

Thoughtfully she ran her comb through her glossy chestnut hair. What was she to make of

Kurt's attitude towards her? More significantly, what was she to make of her own conflicting feelings? The second question flashed into her mind before she had time to ponder on the first.

Abandoning it without finding an answer, she went into the hall where Kurt and Isobel stood talking.

'By the way,' Isobel said as she saw them out, 'I give a ten per cent discount in my shop to friends. Call in some time when you're in town and have a browse round.'

'Thanks for the offer,' Kurt said. 'You don't sell hand-embroidered blouses by any chance?'

'No, I'm afraid you're out of luck. I deal in wickerwork.'

'There's a very good embroidery shop in the Rua da Alfandega,' Rosalind told him.

She was proud of her voice that betrayed none of the angry jealousy inside her. She was sure that the present was intended for Vivienne.

'I must make a point of going there. My sister will be very disappointed if I don't bring her back a hand-embroidered blouse,' Kurt said, a trace of humour in his tone.

Rosalind's jealousy melted away. She remembered Kurt's sister, Stephanie, who must by now be a teenager. She'd rather envied him coming from such a large family. Stephanie, being the only girl with four older brothers, had learned early how to twist them round her little finger, and undoubtedly she'd extracted a promise of a blouse from Kurt the moment she knew he was coming to Madeira.

In the car Kurt commented as he pulled away from the kerb, 'I fancy there's a touch of jealousy at work there.'

'What?' Rosalind's startled question drew his gaze.

'Isobel,' he explained. 'From what she was saying to me while you were changing, I gather she's very anxious to have the new house completed so you and Julia can live there and she can have your father to herself. What did you think I meant?'

'I...nothing,' she lied. For an unnerving moment she thought he'd guessed she was still emotionally involved with him enough to be jealous of his mistress.

Again her senses warned her of a slicingly keen blue glance slanted in her direction, but he didn't challenge her reply. Instead he asked, 'When's the date of their wedding?'

'Dad hasn't even asked Isobel to marry him yet,' she answered.

'She's jumping the gun a bit, isn't she?'

'You mean in wanting me out of the house?'

'That—and men usually like to do the proposing,' Kurt amplified.

'Isobel feels Dad *would* do the proposing if it weren't for me. At least that's what she said this afternoon.'

'Has she been giving you a rough time?' he asked.

She knew from his voice that he was frowning.

'No rougher than you've been giving me,' she murmured darkly.

'I wouldn't have said a few minor skirmishes constituted rough treatment,' he shot back.

'I don't want to argue with you.'

'Nicely dodged,' he applauded drily and then prompted, 'You were saying about Isobel.'

'I understand how she feels,' Rosalind said. 'If I loved a man I'd want him to myself.'

She sensed the flicker of his blue gaze and threaded her fingers together in her lap. Why did there always have to be undercurrents when they talked. Without them she had the feeling that, despite the past, they might have succeeded in being friends.

'And have you ever been in love?' he asked, his inflexion sardonic.

A knife-thrust of angry pain went through her. She masked it with a cool, 'I was with you once, believe it or not.'

'I'd like to believe it.'

She turned her head towards him. If only the veil could be lifted from her eyes even for a second so that she could see his expression and know how to interpret his words. The frustrations of being blind had multiplied a hundredfold since he had come back into her life.

'And I'd like to believe you were once in love with me, but that would be too naïve,' she answered.

She had the impression of a dark brow quirked at her.

'Even the most ardent devotion has its limits,' he muttered.

The sun-roof of the Mercedes was open and with the noise of the traffic and the breeze that blew her hair back from her face she missed his remark.

'What did you say?' she asked.

'Forget it,' he answered. Changing the topic, he went on, 'By the way, if you want to go to the fiesta Isobel was talking about you're welcome to come with me.'

Surprised by his invitation, Rosalind fought a battle with herself. Part of her wanted to accept it.

Another part of her warned against being exposed to the force of his masculine charm.

'Won't you find I stop you enjoying the fun?' she asked. 'With all the crowds I wouldn't dare to let go of you for a minute.'

'That's fine by me.'

A crease of puzzlement appeared between her brows. Why did her blindness seem not to bother him now, when two years ago it had been the cause of the break-up of their relationship? She reminded herself it had been the hereditary factor above all that he had been unable to accept, and then of course there had been Vivienne in the background.

Taken up with her thoughts, she was fractionally later than she would have been otherwise in realising that they weren't heading towards the *quinta*. The rumble of the other traffic and the smooth purr of her father's Mercedes told her that, whichever road they were driving along, it wasn't the one that climbed up away from Funchal.

'Where are you taking me?' she asked.

'Afraid I might be abducting you?' came the mocking reply.

To her chagrin she coloured slightly. The sensual note in his voice, apart from the idea itself, was enough to quicken her heartbeat.

'I'm just curious as to where we're going,' she said, and hoped she fooled him into thinking she felt as calm and unruffled as she sounded.

'Into the centre of Funchal. I've got a couple of letters to post, remember?' he told her. 'I need to get stamps for them. Do you want to wait for me in the car—I won't be long—or will you come with me to the Post Office?'

'I'll come with you,' she said.

Her answer was made without hesitating. It jolted her a little. She could only think that her desire for Kurt's company stemmed from the fact that the mood between them had altered. Inexplicably his mockery had lost its corrosive edge and the rapport that had once existed between them was coming to the fore.

You're dicing with danger, an inner voice told her. Kurt all but destroyed you once and he'll destroy you again if you let him. She refused to listen. In the last two days she'd felt more alive than she had in the last two years.

She found her cane, which was propped up beside her legs, and got out of the car, declining Kurt's offer to take his arm.

'I like to manage on my own,' she explained.

'So I've notice,' he answered, a humorous inflexion in his husky voice.

She was adept at negotiating static objects, but fast-moving traffic and people interweaving on the pavement, some meandering by, others bustling past, presented a much greater problem. Her grip tightened determinedly on her white cane as a flutter of timidity affected her pulse. Invariably she felt unsure of herself away from the known territory of the *quinta* and its gardens.

The blast of a ship's hooter in the harbour startled her, as did the scream of brakes as a van drew up in a hurry and the driver leapt out, slamming the door. It was frightening to have no visual warning of any sound, no coherent mental picture of what was around her. Though she wasn't aware of it, she slowed her pace. She was beginning to wish she had elected to stay safely in the car, when Kurt tucked her hand through his arm.

'Be careful along here,' he warned. 'There are steps ahead.'

'Up or down?' she asked drawing a steadying breath.

The mêlée of noise from all around wasn't nearly as bewildering with his muscular forearm as solid as rock beneath her fingers.

'Down,' he told her. An attractive note of self-mockery in his voice, he joked, 'I forgot to mention that important fact.'

'Then it was just as well I thought to ask,' she quipped in return, 'or I might have fallen down the whole flight.'

'Don't worry, I'd have picked you up at the bottom.'

'How very reassuring!' Her laughter was so spontaneous that she surprised not only him but herself.

'That's a nice sound,' he commented. 'I don't think I've heard you laugh till now.'

'You need to feel at ease with someone to laugh with them.'

'Should I be encouraged by that comment?' he asked, teasing her.

'All I meant was I haven't lost my sense of humour,' she stated, wondering what she had given away with her previous remark.

'Let's just say that until now you've kept it well hidden while I'm around.'

'Perhaps...' she began.

'Perhaps what?' he prompted as she broke off.

But she had thought better of her reply. To answer that she hadn't wanted memories awoken of how well her sense of humour interlocked with his would be too telling. Instead she murmured, 'Perhaps I'm finding you easier to get along with.'

'How far is it to Isobel's shop from here?' he asked as they emerged from the cool interior of the Post Office into the sunlight again.

'About five minutes' walk.'

'Shall we stroll along to it?' he suggested.

'Why not?' she agreed.

Giving into the impulse, she slipped her hand through his arm. Then, sensing the glance he slanted her, she challenged, 'Well?'

'Well, what?'

'I thought you were about to make some comment on the fact that I've chosen to take your arm.'

'It did come as something of a surprise,' he stated, adding, 'For someone so calm and quiet you're very strong-willed.'

'I can't be a model of all the virtues.'

Her pert answer drew an amused bark of laughter in response. With Kurt guiding her she didn't have to give her attention to the bustle on the pavements, which made it easier for her to give her attention to their conversation.

Isobel's shop was doing a brisk trade. A coach had drawn up outside and tourists, keen to buy, were examining the array of baskets that were of every shape and size. In the cobbled courtyard a display of wickerwork garden loungers, stools and chairs was set out and they, too, were being much admired.

'I didn't expect we'd find it so crowded,' Rosalind murmured as they went inside. 'I'm afraid to move in case I start an avalanche of bread baskets!'

'At least they're not breakable,' Kurt chuckled. His tanned arm went round her. 'Squeeze in. Someone's trying to come past with a garden chair.'

Any physical contact with him, no matter how impersonal, was a reminder of his maleness. He drew her closer as footsteps approached. Her heartbeat quickened as she felt the hardness of his thighs against hers. The aroma of his aftershave was spicy, a disturbingly masculine fragrance, while the strength of the arm that encircled her waist made her feel like a fluttering fledgeling captured.

She moistened her lips nervously as the tourist lumbered past with a friendly, 'Gee, but these aisles are narrow!'

As soon as he'd gone past Kurt released her.

'I thought you were going to squash me,' she said, a husky catch in her voice despite the laughter in it.

She hoped the explanation for her breathlessness sounded more convincing to his ears than it did to hers. From his answer seemingly it did.

'Sorry,' he laughed in reply. She heard him pick up one of the skilfully stacked objects. 'Whoever would want an exact replica of a garden watering can made of wickerwork, I wonder?' he said.

'It's not meant to be practical,' she said, smiling at his tone of quizzical amusement. 'It's simply decorative—a demonstration of the weaver's craft. If you look you'll see that no wires, glue or nails are used even in the most complicated items.'

'Where are the articles made?' he asked.

'In people's homes,' she said, visualising the baskets he was looking at, his hands strong and capable as they examined the high standard of workmanship. 'Basket-making, even today, is a cottage industry on Madeira. It reflects its beginnings as a simple task to occupy people's time in the winter when there wasn't so much to do on the land.'

'You make it sound like a form of therapy.'

'I think working with your hands often is.'

'Is that spoken from the heart?' he said.

'Why should I need therapy?' she asked.

'As an outlet for frustrations of being blind.'

'I've told you I'm not frustrated,' she insisted coolly.

'There's no need to drop the temperature to zero suddenly,' Kurt mocked. 'I wasn't referring to sexual frustration.'

Rather than dignify his taunt by rising to it, she said, 'If you've finished looking round here, would you like me to show you where the embroidery shop is?'

'You're very clever at finding your way about,' he commented. 'How do you do it?'

'It's practice,' she explained. 'I know the number of blocks to get to where I want to go.'

'You mean you count them?'

She nodded. 'If I didn't I'd soon get lost.'

At the shop on the Rua da Alfandega Kurt soon picked out a blouse he liked. 'What do you think of this one?' he asked Rosalind as he handed the hanger to her.

'What colour is it?' she asked.

'Pale aquamarine, but that's as much as I'm going to tell you.'

She smiled, accepting the challenge. Her fingers told her that the blouse was in cool silk. It had a mandarin collar and daintily embroidered front, fastening with silk-covered buttons. She described it aloud and then said, 'It's beautiful, but it's a bit sophisticated for Stephanie. At her age, I think, she'd rather have a brightly embroidered camisole.'

'Yes, I think she would,' Kurt agreed. 'I wasn't intending buying this blouse for her. I had someone else in mind.'

Rosalind's mouth tightened. The aquamarine blouse would complement Vivienne's ash-blonde hair and cool Nordic looks perfectly.

'Let me guess,' she said coolly.

'If you're wrong it's a forfeit.' His mocking answer was sardonic.

'I don't think I shall be,' she returned, 'since doubtless you're still carrying a torch for Vivienne.'

'That's one forfeit you owe me,' Kurt answered silkily, 'but I'll collect payment at a more appropriate time.'

An alarmingly pleasant shiver traced down her spine.

'Then... Then who...?' she began in confusion, wishing she had held her tongue.

'I'm buying the blouse for you,' Kurt informed her.

'For me? But... why?' she faltered.

'So you can wear it at the fiesta.'

'I've got heaps of pretty clothes I could——'

'I'm sure you have, but I wouldn't advise arguing,' he warned, cutting her protest short.

She couldn't think why he should want to buy her a present, but fingering the delicate silk and knowing she would treasure the blouse, she answered with an engagingly mischievous smile, 'Then I'll accept it as a peace offering.'

Kurt payed for the two blouses and they left the shop, stopping at a café with tables set out under parasols for a cappuccino before returning to the car. As they arrived back at the *quinta* and went inside the house he said, 'Why not straight to it, then?'

'Straight to what?' she asked, her pulse jumping nervously as his forfeit flashed through her mind.

'Your studio, of course. You promised me a look round the citadel.'

'What makes you call it the citadel?' she asked.

'It seemed appropriate.'

'I don't retreat from our skirmishes there, if that's what you're implying,' she said as he took her arm to lead her across the tiled hall.

'Is that a fact?' he gibed softly.

'Yes, as it happens,' she answered, opening the door to her studio and allowing him inside.

She guessed from the silence that he was looking around him. His pantherish tread told her the display of figures in the glass cabinet on the far wall had caught his attention. If her studio was a citadel, she thought, then she had let the enemy in through the gates just as the Trojans had welcomed in the wooden horse.

'Where did you get the inspiration for these?' he asked.

'Do you mean the Inca-style figures?' she guessed.

'Yes,' he confirmed.

'Like you, I'm interested in Peruvian culture,' she said. 'I really envy you your trekking holiday in the Andes.'

There was the sound of the glass front of the cabinet being opened.

'You've captured all the vigour and spontaneity of the early Inca art,' he remarked, taking one of the strong squat fingers from the shelf to look at it more closely.

She was now beginning to reap the acclaim of the art world, yet even so she felt a glow of pleasure at Kurt's endorsement of her work.

'I wanted to experiment with something different,' she answered. 'A lot of my sculptures are of animals.'

'So I see.'

From the direction of his voice he had moved to look at the studies she had made when she'd been working on a composition entitled 'Lion Cubs at Play'.

'These are fascinating,' he said.

'They're a sort of record of how the final sculpture took shape. I worked out my ideas for it using the clay sketches you're looking at and then...' she laughed '...I couldn't bear to throw them away.'

'Who has the finished sculpture?'

'It was commissioned for the lobby of a safari lodge in Kenya.'

'Very appropriate,' Kurt told her. 'And what are you working on now?'

'A mother and child. It's on the work bench if you want to take a look at it.'

She heard the faint rustling of plastic as he unwrapped the sculpture.

'You go from strength to strength,' he murmured, clearly impressed by the eloquence of her work.

The eloquence was all the greater in the sculpture of mother and child because unconsciously she had expressed in it all her feelings about motherhood.

The child on the woman's lap was Kurt's child, the child she would never have.

'I'll have it finished before you leave,' she said. 'Since you've given me a present, perhaps you'll accept one from me.'

She had decided previously that she wouldn't exhibit the figure of mother and child, that she would keep it for herself. Yet now she was offering it to Kurt, and from her casual tone he would never guess that strangely it was like giving away part of herself.

'Ironic that you should create such a tender picture of motherhood.' Kurt's voice was abrasive.

If he had hit her she couldn't have felt more pain. She had been forced to give up all her dreams of having a baby and now, when they appeared to be getting on, he suddenly threw the fact in her face with more cruelty than she would have believed possible. She clutched at the work bench to steady herself.

Then came the tornado of anger. It was as if something inside her suddenly snapped, exploding her calm, unshatterable self-control into a myriad white hot fragments. Hell-bent on destroying the sculpture which his words had ruined for her, she seized hold of it, a slim, blazing fury. She smashed it down on the work bench and then gave a gasp as, before her fists could inflict any greater damage, Kurt snatched hold of both her wrists.

'What the hell do you think you're doing?' he rasped.

'You bastard!' she sobbed in the grip of emotions so violent that she was shaking with the force of them.

'Have you gone crazy?' he demanded. 'That statue was beautiful!'

'I hope I've smashed it. I hope I've turned it back into nothing but a lifeless lump of clay! How dare you jeer at me about motherhood, twist the knife in the wound? My life was ruined that day I went to the hospital! And you dare taunt me about it as though it were somehow my fault!' Emotion began to choke her voice. 'If I were to regain my sight tomorrow, it couldn't compensate for the fact that my chance of having a child...'

'If you wanted Andrew's child so badly, why didn't you go ahead and have it?' Kurt cut in, his hands that had gripped her wrists moving to take hold of her roughly by the shoulders.

'Andrew's child?' she echoed in bewilderment. 'Why would I want to have a child by Andrew when it was you I was in love with?'

'Don't say you did it for me!' Kurt jeered with contempt.

'Did what?' she stormed.

'Had the abortion to please me.'

She pushed his hands from her shoulders and took a step back. Rocked to the core, it was an instant before she managed to demand in a low, shaking voice, 'Where in God's name did you get the idea from that I had an abortion, that I was ever even pregnant?'

'Playing the innocent because you don't want anyone outside this room to know? If you want to keep up the virginal pretence with Manuel, fine, but it's a little late to pretend with me, when two years ago you not only didn't deny it, you confirmed every word Vivienne said.'

'Vivienne?' It was a whisper of incredulity. 'Are you saying Vivienne told you that...?'

She turned away, so many emotions warring within her that she couldn't continue. She was dizzy, reeling, unable to grasp all the implications of what had apparently been a terrible misunderstanding skilfully engineered by Vivienne.

Kurt's hand as he reached for her was imperative.

'Don't touch me!' she said in a hissing whisper.

Far from complying with her command, he spun her to face him.

'Am I to believe from the shocked way you're acting that Vivienne was lying, that you weren't pregnant with Andrew's child?' he demanded. His fingers bit into her arm. 'Answer me, damn it!'

'How could you even think it was true?' she accused with a telling flash of fire.

She sensed from the rigidity of his stance that for an instant he was stunned.

'Then why the hell did you go along with it?' Angry incomprehension vibrated his voice.

'I didn't go along with anything!' she denied. 'I thought Vivienne had told you I was going blind. I...I thought that once you found that out you didn't want me any more.'

'You mean...you mean you knew you were going blind, then?'

If she'd needed any further confirmation that he hadn't rejected her for the reason she'd always believed, she had it in his thunderstruck inflexion.

CHAPTER EIGHT

'You didn't know!' she breathed almost to herself as the impact of it sank in.

'No, I didn't,' he agreed.

There was very little inflexion in his husky voice, making it impossible for her to guess what he was thinking.

'Then... then how... when did you find out?' she asked.

'Through Julia. When she contacted me in London I naturally asked after you. That was when she told me you'd lost your sight.'

'And all this time I thought...' she whispered.

'Yes, all this time,' he agreed grimly. From the sound of his footsteps he was pacing up and down with leashed frustration. Then he pivoted to explode, 'Why, for God's sake, didn't you tell me? You let me think all kinds of things about you...'

'Things that you were only too ready to believe!' she cut in. The calm interlude of a moment ago was broken as tempers flared again. 'I'd like to know just what story Vivienne spun you!'

'A pretty ugly one,' he muttered.

'Obviously!'

Her angry exclamation made him take hold of her arm, gripping it for emphasis as he shot back, 'And one I'd have dismissed out of hand if you hadn't been showing Andrew out when I drove round to your place that afternoon I arrived back from Toronto!'

'What does Andrew have to do with this?'

'You tell me.' He clipped out the words.

She snatched her arm free.

'As far as I'm concerned he has nothing to do with it!'

'Then why was he at your flat that day?'

'Because I happened to bump into him the previous afternoon.'

'You mean it was pure coincidence?'

'Yes,' she flashed, stung by his scepticism. 'I wasn't carrying on with him behind your back, if that's what you're implying!' Her voice changed as suddenly it occurred to her how Vivienne might have misrepresented things to Kurt. 'Is that...is that what Vivienne claimed?' she faltered. 'Is that why she contacted you the moment you got back from Canada?'

'She left a message for me at Heathrow asking me to call her urgently, which I did,' Kurt answered. 'She said she had some terrible news to give me, news she couldn't tell me over the phone. She had to see me. I found it hard to be patient when she wouldn't give me any inkling of what was wrong. I told her it would take me about an hour to drive home, thinking I'd drive over to see her. Instead she was outside my house in her car, waiting for me, when I pulled up.'

He paused and Rosalind had the impression that he dragged a hand through his black hair before continuing, 'Vivienne's story was that she'd met you the previous day for lunch. When she arrived at the restaurant you were already there deep in conversation with a guy you introduced to her as your ex-boyfriend.'

'So far that's what happened,' Rosalind said. 'Andrew was meeting his parents.'

'According to Vivienne, no sooner had you parted from him than you broke down in tears.' His voice hard, Kurt stated, 'She said you'd sobbed out that you'd only agreed to marry me because after your affair with Andrew was over you'd discovered you were pregnant. Then while I was away things changed. Andrew had decided he wanted you back, but he didn't want the tie of a baby. So because you were still in love with him you agreed to his terms.'

'And you believed her!' Rosalind said torn between disbelief and fury.

'No, damn it, I didn't believe her!' Kurt rasped. 'I threw her out of the house and then came straight over to see you. What I didn't expect was to find you there with Andrew!'

'Which you thought confirmed her story!' Rosalind snapped.

'You were the one who did that.' His clipped voice revealed the tight hold he had on his temper. 'If you remember, you threw my ring back at me and as good as told me you were in love with Andrew.'

'I...' Rosalind turned away, her hand going to her temples in her struggle for composure.

She was only just beginning to comprehend how poisonous and clever Vivienne was. Devastated by the discovery that she was losing her sight, and terribly in need of reassurance from Kurt, she had walked straight into the trap Vivienne had set for her. The moment Kurt had challenged her she had assumed the very worst.

In a cramped whisper she said, 'I...I was so hurt... That was why I pretended I was still in love with Andrew. I wanted to hurt you back to dent your masculine pride.'

'Dent my pride?' he grated, as though he could scarcely credit what she was saying.

'Yes!' she sparked with a flash of spirit as she pivoted to face him again. 'Vivienne told me you wouldn't want me as soon as you knew I was going blind. When you accused me, what she'd said was so uppermost in my thoughts that it never crossed my mind you meant anything else! I'd clung to the belief that you loved me enough for it to make no difference, and then you came round and yelled at me! It seemed to substantiate exactly what Vivienne had told me, that you didn't want a wife who was blind.'

'The spiteful bitch!' Kurt muttered with a savagery that would have made her blood run cold had it been directed at her. 'Why ever didn't you call me in Toronto,' he demanded, 'instead of confiding in Vivienne?'

She moved to the work bench and leant against it. Her squall of temper was spent and her knees felt shaky. She was gathering her strength for a reply when he said, 'Is it too badly damaged to put it right?'

'What?' she breathed in a whisper, her heart jolting with the construction she put on his words.

'The sculpture. I thought you were checking to see what the damage was.'

She realised her hand was almost touching the mangled figure of mother and child.

'I...I don't know,' she said.

Pulling herself together, she drew the sculpture towards her. She didn't know what the state of play was between them. She didn't know she even wanted to know. She felt like a canoeist used to calm waters who had just survived the white, foaming rapids and was now so shaken that she could only rely on instinct to keep her afloat. That instinct warned her to put up every barrier she could think of against his masculinity and charisma.

'Often it's easier to start again than to try to repair what's damaged,' Kurt told her.

'I'm not inclined to do either,' she answered quietly. 'I'd only keep comparing it with what I'd done before and know it wasn't as good.'

Kurt turned her towards him.

'Is that the same attitude you have with regard to you and me?'

'Why... why do you want to know?' she asked.

'I would have thought it was obvious,' he returned with a touch of sarcasm.

'Well, it isn't. Any more than it's obvious what was going on between you and Vivienne.'

'I thought I'd explained about Vivienne.' His tone was impatient.

'You explained the lies she told us both, not what your relationship with her was.'

'When are you going to learn to trust me?' he demanded.

'Perhaps I might if I could look into your eyes,' she said. 'Since I can't I have to rely on instinct.'

'And what does instinct tell you?'

'That Vivienne was and still is your mistress!'

'Your jealousy is very complimentary,' he mocked. 'It suggests things aren't as over between us as you'd like to claim.'

'To be jealous I'd have to be in love with you.'

'And you're telling me you're not.' It was halfway between a statement and a question.

Unsure of him, even had she been able to sort out her chaotic feelings she wouldn't have admitted what they were.

'Not any more,' she told him.

'Your last declaration was that the fire had gone out of our relationship and only the ashes were left.'

His reply recalled the previous night when her response to his kiss had given the lie to her statement.

'I'm not denying I'm still attracted to you,' she said with a blush.

'Then in which case,' he said, moving so that she was pinned against the work bench, 'you won't mind if I collect my forfeit.'

Unable to retreat, she tried to fend him off. Her hands pushed at the strong plane of his chest, the contact her palms made with his powerful man's body making her pulse flutter. 'Kurt, don't,' she whispered without conviction.

'Why not?' he taunted, threading his fingers into her burnished hair as he tilted up her face. 'You've already said you're attracted to me. Just as I'm attracted to you.'

He bent his head, kissing the sensitive pulse that beat at the base of her throat. Imperceptibly she caught her breath, determined not to give in to the sweet sensations that were heating her blood.

She curled her hands into fists. The fragrance of his aftershave was utterly male and as evocative as a half-remembered melody. He nibbled her earlobe, his hands sliding beneath her overshirt to caress her bare skin. She closed her eyes in a last desperate effort to resist.

Kurt raised his head. Trembling, she thought that with her coldness and complete lack of resistance she had won the day. But she was wrong.

'OK, sweetheart, if that's the way you want to play it,' he said softly.

The next instant she found herself pulled tightly against him. She gave a gasp of protest and as she did so Kurt's mouth came down on hers. She began to fight him then, but he was not to be thwarted. He held her possessively, his lips forcing hers to part for the invasion of his.

An agonising dart of pleasure pierced her as his mouth began to plunder hers. The fabric of his shirt was fine, and through it the warmth of his strong man's body teased her breasts. Her nipples tightened in response, a shatteringly erotic sensation.

She stopped fighting him, her hands that had been clenched into fists clutching at his shoulders to steady herself, and then moving in a tentative caress. Kurt's kiss was a blunt statement of desire, its expertise and passion beyond anything she could summon up in resistance.

She forgot that it had been her intention to struggle until he was forced to let her go. Instead her arms wound feverishly round his neck, her body slim and willing as his hands moved lower, holding her yet more intimately. Her mind was closed to everything save the sensation of him, the wild tremors that danced along her nerves.

How long the kiss went on she didn't know, nor what intimacies she might have allowed him had not the door opened at that moment.

'Rosalind,' her aunt began, clearly assuming she was quietly at work in her studio.

With Julia's interruption the spell of the moment shattered. As though his touch suddenly burned her, Rosalind snatched herself out of Kurt's arms. What madness had possessed her, that she had lost control, her senses yielding helplessly to passion?

'Oh! I...I'm sorry. I didn't realise you were with Kurt.' There was surprise in Julia's voice. 'I...I'll come back later.'

The door was closed again quickly.

'Now look what you've done!' Rosalind turned to him, hot colour staining her cheeks.

'Made your aunt's day, I should think,' he returned, amused. 'Why does her matchmaking bother you? It doesn't bother me.'

Any more than having an affair with a married woman had bothered him, she thought!

'No, I don't imagine it does,' she said with a lift of her chin, furious with herself for the warmth she had shown in his arms.

'Who is it you're angry with?' he mocked. 'Me for kissing you, or your aunt for interrupting?'

Her mouth tightened. But refusing to give him the satisfaction of another stormy answer she said, 'If you'll excuse me, I'll go and see what Julia wants.'

'You're all fire one minute and all frost the next.' he shot back. His tone suggested his black brows were lowered in a scowl. 'Just what are you playing at, Rosalind?'

'Survival!' she retorted as she headed for the door.

His hand caught hold of her wrist.

'What do you mean, survival?' he questioned.

At that moment she couldn't have told him. It had been a reflex answer.

'I think you're the one who's playing games,' she accused.

'Do you?' he said drily as he released her. 'Well, console yourself with the thought that, if I am, you've got five more days to try to evade me.'

She took a defensive step back. Conscious of the stab of his gaze, she crossed the hall, making her escape through the drawing-room on to the veranda. She paused there an instant to recover from their sexual sparring.

Uppermost in her mind was the thought that he hadn't rejected her because of her blindness. But that didn't mean all the problems that existed in their relationship were solved. They were no longer talking at cross purposes, yet she was no nearer to understanding where she stood with him.

What did he want? A brief fling with her during the time he was staying at the *quinta*, or did his feelings go deeper than that?

He found her attractive, that much was clear, but physical desire wasn't the same as love. And then there was Vivienne. For her to have acted with such spite and venom, he must have meant a great deal to her. Kurt hadn't denied that she'd been his mistress.

She went down the steps from the veranda and began to walk along the sun dappled path. The banks of hibiscus bushes soon screened her from the view of the house. The gardens were somnolent and peaceful but their tranquillity did little to calm her.

If only she knew what to make of the things he had said to her just now, the way he had kissed her.

Was it possible he was in love with her? Or did Vivienne have a prior claim on his heart? she wondered with a flare of jealousy.

She tried to be rational. She thought of the gentle firmness in his touch when he guided her. That gentleness could easily be ascribed to compassion. It proved nothing, she insisted. And yet there had been nothing compassionate about his mockery. Whatever he felt for her, it wasn't pity.

She sat down on the wicker garden seat that was placed under the shade of a graceful jacaranda. She knew from the ache beneath her ribs that deep down she wanted to let herself think that Kurt was in love with her.

You mustn't think it, she told herself fiercely, the reflex answer she had given him suddenly making sense. Whether Kurt was playing games with her or not, she was fighting a desperate battle for emotional survival where he was concerned.

It was true he wasn't the heartless devil she had once believed. He'd made it clear in her studio that blindness didn't matter to him, but he evidently didn't know it was hereditary. And even without Vivienne to complicate the picture that might matter very much, she thought, her throat tight.

A little miaow of greeting told her that Cleo must have spotted her sitting on the seat. Her Siamese jumped up beside her. Reflectively Rosalind stroked the cat's silky fur, which was hot from the sun.

'Do you realise I'm in exactly the same position I was in two years ago?' she whispered aloud.

It was some time before she stood up to return to the house, unable to bring order to the confusion inside her. Companionably Cleo wandered down the lawn with her, the silver bell on her collar tinkling faintly.

Julia was enjoying the evening sun on the veranda.

'I hoped you'd still be with Kurt,' she began.

Rosalind refrained from commenting that her aunt had made that very obvious. Instead she asked, 'What did you want me for?'

'Only to tell you that Manuel called while you were out. He said he'd stop by later. I think it's about the fiesta.'

'The fiesta?' Rosalind said as she sat down.

'Yes, he asked if we were going. I said probably not. I know you find it frightening to be where there are crowds.'

'I do, but...' it was ironic that, when Kurt's closeness invariably imposed a strain on her pulse, she should feel safe whenever he took her arm to guide her. '...but I...I've agreed to go with Kurt,' she said.

'Have you, indeed?' Julia laughed. 'Well, after that little admission, and the way the two of you were kissing when I walked into your studio, you can't make out now you've no feelings for him.'

'I have plenty of feelings for him,' Rosalind answered. 'Too many to have him treat me as someone to amuse himself with while he's here.'

'You surely can't think that's what he's doing?'

'I don't know what to think,' Rosalind confessed.

'He seems serious enough about you to me,' Julia answered.

'That's because...' Rosalind began. She broke off and started again. 'I'd be tempted to think that too, but I thought he was serious about me two years ago. And then I found out there was someone else. A lot of what Vivienne told me was lies, but she couldn't have caused so much trouble had there been nothing between her and Kurt. And for all I know she may still be important to him.'

'For all you know?' her aunt questioned the phrase she had used. 'Haven't you asked him about her?' she asked gently.

Rosalind nodded. 'Just now when we were in my studio I challenged him about Vivienne.'

'And what did he say?'

'That I'm to trust him.'

'Well, it's not a very satisfactory answer, I'll admit,' Julia conceded. 'But if you love him, fight for him.'

'Against Vivienne? I wouldn't stand a chance.'

'That's a defeatist attitude.'

'It's a realistic attitude. You haven't seen her,' Rosalind said. 'She's sharp, stunning, and sexy.'

'She may be, but so are you,' Julia insisted. 'You're very attractive and you're lively company.'

'I'm also blind.'

'I thought so,' her aunt murmured. 'I thought your blindness was at the bottom of this!'

'I have to face up to the facts,' Rosalind answered. 'I don't know how involved Kurt is with Vivienne, but even if he's not involved with her any more I do know he wants a family. And that raises all sorts of questions, questions I can't deal with. If he is serious about me I'm going to be hurt, and if he's not I'm going to be hurt. And... and to be honest I don't think I can bear to be hurt any more.'

'You're not making any sense, darling,' Julia answered. 'What sort of questions does it raise, Kurt wanting a family? You're very fond of children. You always have been.'

Rosalind bit her lip, determined not to let it tremble. For two years she had buried the deep, awful pain that had been with her from the moment she had learned her eye disease was hereditary.

She drew breath for an answer and then started as she heard the sound of a man's tread. Her aunt patted her hand.

'It's only João,' she said.

'I thought it was Kurt,' she murmured, relieved.

'The lid to the water butt fits like a glove now,' the gardener informed her. 'Cleo won't be able to fall into it again.'

'Thank you, João,' she said appreciatively.

'That reminds me, João,' Julia said, diverted for a moment from her conversation with her niece. 'I wanted to ask whether you know of anyone who'd see to the garden for me when the new house is completed. I know I could advertise, but I'd rather rely on your recommendation.'

'If my nephew has time I'm sure he'd be interested.'

'That would be wonderful. Would you mention it to him for me?'

'It will be my pleasure, *senhora*.' He smiled.

'What a stroke of luck,' Julia announced as his footsteps faded. 'But to get back to you and Kurt.'

Rosalind shook her head.

'Talking about it doesn't seem to help,' she said with a sigh.

'Well,' her aunt said in a kindly tone, 'don't give up. Kurt's here for another five days yet. Anything could happen.'

It was exactly what Rosalind was afraid of.

She kept out of his way until it was time for dinner. She had changed into a stylishly cut cream dress in cool voile. Usually she wore flat pumps to be sure of her footing, but tonight she slipped her feet into high-heeled cream sandals.

Fight for him, her aunt had said. But how could she fight when, even if Kurt was in love with her, she had nothing to offer him. It would take a very special kind of love to accept her as she was, and Vivienne had claimed she would never hold the first place in his heart.

A string of moonstones set in silver completed the pretty picture she made. She wasn't going to fight but nor was she going to concede total defeat to Vivienne. She came on to the galleried landing and then realised that Kurt, too, was on his way downstairs.

'You look very charming this evening,' he said.

'Thank you.'

'No one would ever guess from your cool appearance what a spitfire you can turn into,' he drawled, teasing her gently.

'I like a quiet life,' she smiled. 'I only ever lose my temper when provoked.'

'You lead too quiet a life.'

His criticism hurt a little. As the thought occurred to her she said, 'Is that why you asked me to go to the fiesta with you? Because you feel sorry for me?'

'Don't you think it's time you made up your mind about me? First you decide I'm completely callous. Now you——'

'I never said you were callous,' she protested, cutting in.

'You may not have said it in so many words. But you certainly thought it. If you hadn't been so ready to assume I wouldn't want a wife who was blind, Vivienne couldn't have caused the trouble she did.'

Rosalind reached for the newel post with her hand.

'Equally, had there been nothing between the two of you, she couldn't have caused such trouble,' she retaliated.

'There might be some purpose in continuing this conversation if you trusted me enough to listen,' Kurt muttered. 'But just so you don't end up getting anything else wrong, I didn't ask you to come to the fiesta with me out of pity. Stubborn and wilful though you are, I happen to enjoy your company.'

'That's a back-handed compliment!'

Her indignant reply was greeted by an amused, very masculine chuckle.

'I'll pay you some prettier ones when I've got you alone at the fiesta,' he promised.

His sensual, husky voice reminded her of sensations she was trying to forget. To avoid the touch of his guiding hand on the stairs, she side-stepped, intent on negotiating them without his aide.

Somehow in doing so she missed her footing. She gave a cry as she felt herself falling. Even with his lightning reflexes Kurt was unable to move quickly enough to save her. She tumbled down the full flight of marble stairs.

In the midst of the haze of shock she heard him calling her name.

CHAPTER NINE

WHEN Rosalind came to, a cushion was beneath her head. For a few minutes she lay quite still, her eyes closed, the mantle of sickening blackness too heavy to be thrown off all at once.

There were quick footsteps in the background, Julia talking in an agitated tone from the drawing-room. She had the impression someone was bending over her. The spicy aroma of a man's aftershave brought Kurt into her thoughts.

Slowly she opened her eyes, aware as she did so of a fierce pain shooting through her temples. She realised that a jacket covered her. She tried to stir, the attempt causing a faint moan to escape her lips.

A capable hand enclosed her fingers in its warm, vital grasp.

'Rosalind?' It was Kurt's masculine voice, husky and concerned.

'I...I thought it was you,' she said in a barely audible whisper.

'Don't try to move. Just lie still,' he counselled.

'What...what happened?'

'You've just fallen down the stairs, the whole damned flight.' His tone was clipped.

'I'm sorry,' she murmured in a small voice.

'Sorry? About what?'

'Giving you a scare. That's why you sound angry, isn't it?'

She sensed that her insight took him by surprise.

'I'm only angry that you're hurt,' he answered gently. 'You're very precious to me.'

Or that was what she thought he said. But the blackness was coming over her again in long waves. Her thoughts drifting, she whispered his name. In her dream she imagined he cradled her hand against the roughness of his cheek before pressing a kiss to her palm. And then he was lifting her in his arms.

When she next awoke she was in bed and she could tell there was sunshine flooding into the room. In the quietness a chaffinch was singing. Tentatively she put her hand up to her head, not surprised to find a tender bruise just above her temple.

The door opened and she heard Julia's stealthy footsteps.

'There's no need to tiptoe,' she smiled. 'I'm wide awake.'

'So I see. And you've some colour in your cheeks. Goodness, but you frightened me last night!'

'I frightened myself,' Rosalind admitted. 'It's no fun falling down the stairs.'

'Are you very stiff?'

'Yes, but it will wear off once I've been up for a while.'

'Oh, no, you don't.' Julia pushed her back against the pillows. 'You're not getting out of bed. The doctor said you were to rest.'

'When did the doctor come?' Rosalind asked, startled.

'Last night. I was so glad Kurt was here.'

'Kurt,' she murmured, hazy recollections returning of his bending over her when she had first come round.

'Yes, he took care of you while I phoned for the doctor,' Julia explained.

'I... I think I remember,' she said. 'I... I was lying at the foot of the stairs.'

'That's right. Kurt wouldn't move you until he'd checked first to make sure you hadn't broken any bones.'

'He checked me over?' The idea was vaguely disturbing.

'Yes, and then he carried you up to your room.'

A slight furrow creased Rosalind's brow. Very dimly there was the recollection of being held against his chest as he mounted the stairs before he laid her gently on the bed.

'Do you feel you could eat some lunch?' Julia asked, breaking into her thoughts.

'It can't be lunchtime!'

'You've been asleep a long time,' Julia smiled. 'The doctor gave you a sedative.'

'I'm not terribly hungry,' Rosalind admitted. 'But I'd love a cup of tea. And... and I'd like to say thank you to Kurt. Is he about?'

'He's working on some drawings downstairs. I'll tell him you're awake.'

As her aunt went out Rosalind sat up carefully, pushing the pillow behind her back. It was something of a miracle, she realised, that she hadn't cracked a rib. Meaning to investigate the extent of her bruises, she slid her hand across her ribcage.

It was the silky fabric of her nightgown which reminded her of how low cut it was despite its pretty inset of lace. As she heard Kurt's quick lithe tread on the landing she groped hurriedly for her wrap, abandoning her flustered search as her bedroom door opened.

'What are you hunting for?' Kurt asked.

'My... my wrap.'

'Are you cold?' There was a trace of amusement in his voice.

'No, of course not,' she stammered.

'Then why do you want your wrap?'

Had she been able to see the appreciative glint in his blue eyes as they travelled over her, she couldn't have been been more reminded of her femininity. Unsettled by his gaze, she said, sparking a little, 'You know perfectly well why!'

'Such modesty,' he teased.

As he spoke he put her wrap around her shoulders. Her heart skipped several beats in response to his nearness. Then the mattress dipped as he sat down on the bed and took her hand.

'How are you feeling now?' he asked.

'Bruised, but otherwise OK,' she said with a smile.

'Good.' His hand gave her a squeeze before releasing it.

'You remember when we were in Funchal yesterday afternoon?' she mused.

'Yes.'

'I didn't know, when you said I didn't have to worry about falling down that flight of steps because you'd pick me up at the bottom, that I was going to take you up on the offer so soon.'

'Well, don't take me up on it again.' Despite the quip he was serious. 'You might not be so lucky next time.'

'I know,' she whispered, more shaken from her fall than she was prepared to admit.

* * *

She didn't get up until the evening. She heard the doorbell chime as she was crossing the hall and went to answer it.

'Hello, Rosalind.' The baritone voice was instantly recognisable as Manuel's. 'How are you?' he asked.

'Apart from the odd bruise, I'm fine,' she smiled.

'Well, you're certainly an advertisement for Julia's nursing.'

'Thank you,' she laughed. 'I've been looked after very well.'

'I'm glad to hear it.'

'What's this?' she asked, pleased and surprised as he handed her the flowers he had brought. 'You're not spoiling me, too?' she said.

'I know how you love the scent of carnations and I thought after your tumble downstairs you might be in need of cheering up.'

'How sweet of you.' She laid the cellophane-wrapped carnations on the console table near the door. 'I'll ask Maria to put them in water for me in just a minute. Meanwhile come on in.'

Chatting with him, she led the way into the drawing-room where Julia was absorbed with her embroidery.

'What's this you're working on?' Manuel asked with friendly interest as he sat down beside Julia on the sofa.

'It's a copy of a sampler,' came the answer.

The pause in the conversation told Rosalind that Julia was spreading out her embroidery for Manuel to admire.

'It's delightful,' he said. 'Let me guess. It's for the new house.'

'Maybe,' Julia replied, a smile in her voice. 'Or maybe it's a present for someone. When you said how much you liked the last embroidery picture I worked, I thought I'd make one for you.'

Rosalind, who'd wondered fleetingly before if it was as much her aunt as herself that Manuel was calling round to see, listened to the exchange with interest.

'Will you excuse me? I must go and find Maria,' she said, glad to use the flowers Manuel had brought for her as a pretext to leave him and her aunt together.

As she went in search of the housekeeper she thought how nice it would be if Julia discovered she was in love with Manuel. Thoughtful and steady, he was just the man to keep an eye on her, his masculine firmness complementing her sparkle and caprice.

Amused with herself, Rosalind smiled softly. She'd accused Julia of matchmaking and now she was being just as bad. Perhaps it was catching!

She didn't reflect again on her aunt's friendship with Manuel until the following evening when she came downstairs into the hall that was full of the scent of his carnations. Julia had sounded very animated when she had left for the fiesta with him just a short while before.

Rosalind's own feelings about the evening ahead were more mixed. Apprehension and anticipation fought an inner battle at the thought of sharing in the carnival atmosphere.

Had the saint's day been a week earlier she would almost certainly have chosen to stay at the *quinta*. But her mettlesome nature seemed to have come out of hiding in the last few days. The person responsible for that was Kurt. The sparks he struck off her had somehow given her back her spirit.

'You look charming, *senhorita*.' Maria's voice as she came into the hall was approving. 'What a lovely blouse!'

It was the blouse Kurt had given her. She had teamed it with a plain white skirt that flared gracefully from a smoothly fitting V-shaped basque. Her hair was in a silky top-knot. Tiny aquamarine earrings sparkled on either side of her face, making her look prettier than ever.

'All you need is a flower to wear,' Maria went on. Taking one of the carnations from the vase, she snapped its stem. 'I've nowhere to put it,' Rosalind laughed.

'Tuck it in the waistband of your skirt,' the housekeeper told her, adding, 'Your purse is on the hall table. It will slip in your skirt pocket and your cane's here in the stand when you want it.'

'I...I may not take my cane with me tonight.'

She would have Kurt to guide her, and, although her blindness didn't seem to matter to him, out of a kind of vanity she didn't want to advertise the fact that she could not see. Kurt was tall, goodlooking and arresting even in a crowd. She was too sensitive to want to be identified as the blind girl on his arm.

Her pulse fluttering a little, she walked into the drawing-room. Kurt was smoking and she wondered for how long after he had left the island the waft of a cigar's fragrance would conjure him up painfully in her thoughts.

'I...I'm ready,' she announced.

'The carnation at your waist is a nice touch.' There was a dry tone in his voice as he stubbed out the cigar. He got to his feet. 'Is it to encourage Manuel?'

On edge, she was quick to snap, 'Your mocking cracks are a constant reminder of why it's impossible for us to have any kind of meaningful friendship!'

'I seem to have touched a nerve.'

Although she was nervous about going to the fiesta, she had been looking forward to it. Now Kurt's sarcasm suggested that, far from enjoying the carnival atmosphere, they would be sparring all the time.

To answer him would only give him more ammunition for his next gibe. Her mouth a defiant line, she headed for the door.

'And where do you think you're going?' His tone was dangerously mild.

'To my studio,' she said shortly. Her inner radar warned her that he had moved to intercept her. She visualised him standing in front of her, his feet placed slightly apart in a stance that suggested readiness and arrogance. 'I've changed my mind about going to the fiesta.'

'Is that because your fall downstairs has robbed you of your confidence, or is your change of mind due to Manuel?'

'Manuel has nothing to do with it!'

'Then you don't object to his defection?' Despite his sardonic tone, she had the impression of blue eyes narrowed keenly on her face.

'I'm only too happy to see him and Julia together, if that's what you're referring to,' she retorted.

'That's not the impression you're giving.'

'Just because I'm wearing one of Manuel's carnations,' she said, sparking in spite of herself, 'it doesn't mean I'm in love with him! He's a friend and he's very sweet but that's all there is to it.'

'Well, that makes things a little clearer,' Kurt said. 'Now let's see if we can clarify them even further.'

'What do you mean?'

'Sit down.'

'Why should I?'

'Are you deliberately being difficult?' he frowned, 'or does it come naturally?'

'I'm not going to the fiesta,' she repeated stubbornly, but she sat down anyway.

Kurt's temper had a long fuse, but she knew from the tone that, unjust though it might be, she was trying his patience.

'We'll discuss the fiesta in a minute,' he said. 'Right now we're going to talk about Vivienne.'

She felt a blade-sharp stab of jealousy. If it was true that Vivienne had been his mistress two years ago she would be too angry to forgive him. She curled her fingers into her palms, realising suddenly that she would rather not know.

'I ... I don't want to hear,' she said tightly.

'You're going to hear whether you want to or not,' he ground back.

'You can't make me!'

'Can't I?' he said grimly.

'I suppose if I try to move you'll pin me down,' she said with a last flash of defiance.

'If I have to,' he agreed. 'Vivienne's come between us for quite long enough. You already know we were at university together, that I was dating her.'

'Yes.' The hurt murmur was all she could manage.

'Vivienne was sharp, amusing and good company and I was fascinated by her.'

Rosalind's nails began to make red crescents in her palms. Why was he doing this to her? He was upping the torment of jealousy a thousandfold by talking about his feelings for the other woman.

'And then one day I made the mistake of introducing her to Bradley.'

'So you were in love with her,' Rosalind accused in a cramped whisper.

'A long time ago,' he told her. 'At nineteen you're not always the best judge of character. I didn't realise then what a gold-digger Vivienne was. When she discovered Bradley's father was in property, a millionaire several times over, I wasn't in with a chance.

'Bradley and I had been friends since we were kids at school. Since Vivienne had chosen him and not me, there was no point being a poor loser. The three of us stayed friends. Looking back, I think Vivienne rather liked the sense of power it gave her to imagine I was still in love with her.'

'You mean... Are you saying you stopped loving her?' she asked, not daring to hope.

'Yes,' he said, adding, 'It made things much easier for me. I couldn't have been a visitor at Bradley's house after they were married if I had fancied his wife. I'd have had no option but to drop him.'

'Go on,' Rosalind prompted. Her fingers unclenched to interlace in her lap.

'After my career took off, Vivienne must have decided she'd made the wrong choice. Shortly after I met you at the gallery she pretty well threw herself at me.

'She came round to my house one evening—Bradley was away at the time—told me she was going to leave him and seemed to think I'd jump at the chance to take her to bed and then marry her.

'When she found out she was wrong she burst into tears. She insisted it had been an aberration. She said her marriage had hit a bad patch and that if Bradley so much as even suspected what an utter fool she'd made of herself with me, he'd walk out on her. Had I gone off the air suddenly, Bradley would presumably have wanted to know why. So, because Vivienne had begged me not to jeopardise her marriage and I knew Bradley would expect to meet you, I invited the two of them over for drinks that evening.'

Rosalind didn't answer. She couldn't. She believed him, and the intense trembling relief and happiness inside her made her too choked to speak.

Kurt mistook her silence for disbelief. He strode over to the sofa and pulled her to her feet.

'For God's sake!' he exclaimed. 'Can't you see that the reason Vivienne lied to both of us was out of spite? I'd rejected her and she was determined to have her revenge for that.'

'Why didn't you explain all this before?' Rosalind said, the catch of joy in her voice telling him everything. 'Why did you let me go on thinking, even after that row we had in my studio, that Vivienne was your mistress?'

His hands slid down her arms in a caress, drawing her to his chest.

'I wanted to make you jealous,' he answered. 'I was determined to prove to you one way or another that our relationship wasn't over.'

The note of purpose in his tone filled her with delight.

'You're only staying a week and we've wasted half of it fighting,' she lamented with a little laugh deep in her throat.

'But we're wasting no more.' It was said as a passionate murmur as he framed her face.

She felt her pulse leap as for an instant he held her at the mercy of his gaze. Although she couldn't see, she knew that the eyes that searched hers were a tender, glittering blue, just as intuition told her the moment his gaze travelled to her mouth.

Her cheeks flushed with warmth. In every inch of her she sensed his face moving closer. Her lips parted, a shock of pleasure going through her as he claimed her mouth with his.

The kiss began gently. It was almost as though he were tasting her for the first time. Magical colours rainbowed behind her closed eyes as his lips parted hers in teasing exploration.

Then his arms went round her strongly, moulding her slender form to the hard length of his body. Shivers of delight quivered down her spine as he caressed her. She cupped the back of his neck with her palm, a husky moan escaping her as he deepened the kiss which was passionate, unquenchable, heady as wine.

Aflame with desire, she tangled her fingers into the raven thickness of his hair. Deprived of her sight as she was, her other senses had sharpened, making her thrillingly aware of his rugged virility. Everything about him was overpoweringly male: the spicy scent of his skin, the breadth of his shoulders, the strong arms that held her so possessively. Loving him, wanting him, she was intoxicated.

With a groan Kurt finally raised his head.

'Nectar,' he breathed, holding her to him fiercely.

She murmured his name, and then as he released her a little she reached up to touch his face. He stood quite still as if understanding that her intention was to 'see' him in the only way a blind person could see.

Her sensitive fingers explored his chiselled features, the craggy brow, the strong cheekbones and equally strong jutting jaw. The line of his mouth was as sensuous as his kiss had been. Her heart skipped a beat as she traced his lips with her forefinger. He caught the tip of it gently between his teeth, making her laugh.

'I've wanted to do that ever since you arrived,' she confessed.

'Have I changed much?' he said, his inflexion amused.

'No, you're the same handsome devil I fell in love with two years ago,' she answered, the trembling joy inside her curving her lips into an enchanting smile.

Kurt caught his breath imperceptibly. 'And you're the same red-headed witch, only lovelier,' he muttered, bending to her mouth again.

She melted into his embrace, and when at last his lips left hers it was to return to enjoy a series of small sipping kisses.

'I think we'd better go to the fiesta,' he growled.

'I...I guess you're right,' she said laughingly. 'Oh, Kurt,' she breathed, 'I'm so happy.'

'Me too,' Kurt said, dropping one last kiss on her mouth. 'So let's go and join in the fun.'

It was only a short drive to the pretty mountain village on the outskirts of Funchal where the fiesta was being held. Rosalind smiled as Kurt took her arm, his palm covering her hand which rested on his sleeve.

'Are you worried I might run away?' she joked.

'Let's just say I'm taking no chances,' he chuckled.

The narrow sloping streets were crowded with people and decked with flags and flowers. Agapanthus and hydrangeas filled the air with their heavy perfume and in the background was the sound of a brass band.

She knew already that Kurt had an expert touch when it came to guiding her. Now, as he described the arches of flowers under which they passed, the thronged streets and the fireworks that exploded overhead, she realised what a gift he had for painting pictures with words. It was as if he knew instinctively how to make the whole scene come alive for her.

When they ran into Julia and Manuel, Kurt's arm was around her waist and at his insistence she was trying to guess which flowers were entwined in the arch that spanned the street.

'Look at those rockets!' Julia gasped as there was a sudden whoosh.

'We'll get a better view from the square,' Manuel said.

'Won't it be packed?' her aunt questioned.

'Let's go and see,' Manuel suggested.

'You go ahead. We'll wait here till the procession's gone by. It won't be so crowded,' Kurt told them.

'Are you afraid I might get jostled, or do you want to be alone with me?' Rosalind teased when Manuel and her aunt had moved away.

'I'll have you to myself on the drive back,' he reminded her wickedly, his sensual tone making her pulse quicken. 'Is that a maidenly blush?' he asked.

She slapped him playfully and then gave a little gasp of laughter as his arms tightened round her in a hug.

The gaiety of the fiesta seemed mirrored by the happiness inside her, a happiness that was all the more precious because, like the fragile blossoms which decorated the streets, it was transient. She didn't want to delve into her feelings, to work out why her heart told her to make the most of tonight. She only knew that every moment she shared with Kurt must be lived to the full.

The murmur that ran through the crowd told her when the procession was coming. There was a sudden surge as people pushed to get a glimpse of it. Without meaning to, Rosalind let go of Kurt's hand.

Terrified, she felt herself being swept forward. In the midst of the confusion and jostling, she heard him call her name. The music was coming nearer. Her toe hit a step. She stumbled, her hand that flew out to save her encountering a gatepost. She clung to it, trembling with fright.

The next instant a strong hand grabbed her arm and Kurt's voice broke into her panic.

'Are you OK?' he asked quickly.

She nodded, fighting hard to get a grip on herself. She realised that they hadn't been separated for more than a few seconds. She was perfectly safe. It was fear that had made her imagine she was lost in the crush. 'I...I panicked for an instant when I let go of you,' she answered. 'I...I'm fine.'

'You're shaking like a leaf,' he said, contradicting her.

'I'm okay, honestly,' she insisted. The sound of his voice, that was as resolute as his personality, was steadying her already. Managing a smile she went on, quickly recovering her confidence, 'Don't let's miss the procession.'

Even had she not been blind she wouldn't have caught much more than a glimpse of it above all the heads, but Kurt, being six feet two, was able to see well. As the music faded he said, 'Shall we stay longer or shall we go and have a drink in Funchal?'

'A drink in Funchal would be nice,' she agreed.

With his guiding hand at her elbow they returned to where he had parked the car. The evening was warm and sultry and Kurt drove with the sun-roof open.

She was familiar with every curve and bend of the road which climbed the hillside, yet as a sharp twist gave yet another glimpse of Funchal she said impulsively, 'Pull over and let's stop for a while. You're good with words. I want you to describe the view for me.'

'No, now it's your turn,' Kurt told her.

'My turn?' she queried, smiling back as he drew in by the side of the road.

'Yes. I described the fiesta for you. Now let's see what you can do on your own.'

'OK,' she agreed, accepting his challenge.

She threaded her fingers together in her lap, visualising the scene in her mind. Then she said slowly, 'I think the sky is a deep, deep blue, studded with diamonds scattered against a velvet-dark background. More lights are shining from the cruise ships in the harbour, shimmering across the inky water.' She broke off, suddenly feeling self-conscious. Bewitched by the romance of the evening, she probably sounded ridiculous.

'Why have you stopped?' he demanded.

'I ... I may have got it all wrong,' she said with a laugh.

'You haven't. The evening's every bit as beautiful as you make it sound,' Kurt told her. Picking up where she had left off he went on, 'Where the lights of Funchal finally peter out against the hillside the slopes are all shadowy and indistinct. The pine forests are dark and tranquil and the leaves of the eucalyptus are stirring gently even though there's scarcely a breeze.'

'I can hear them,' she whispered.

'It's a perfect evening for lovers,' he said, his voice a husky murmur as his hand cradled her cheek.

Excitement tingled in her blood as he bent to her mouth. Her lips parted willingly under his, a quiver of fierce pleasure going through her. Their kiss was long and drugging. Her murmur of regret as his lips left hers turned to a sighing moan as they traced the contours of her face and then found the sensitive hollow of the throat.

Desire was a fever heating her skin. She murmured his name and as she did so he found her mouth again. Constantly in her heart was the knowledge that she must savour this night. She kissed him back with a sweet urgency, adding fuel to the fire of their passion.

Her blouse, aided by Kurt's knowing hands, had come untucked from her waistband. His palms slid up her spine as he caressed her warm, naked back. She tightened her grip on his shoulders as the pleasure intensified and then broke the kiss with a gasp as his hands cupped her breast.

He brushed his thumb over the aching tautness of her nipple. His thumb continuing to tantalise the aroused peak, he kissed her once more. When finally he raised his head she was dizzy and trembling.

'Let's go back to the house, sweetheart.' His voice was throaty and unsteady and she knew exactly what he meant.

Wanting him just as much as he wanted her, she whispered,

'Yes.'

CHAPTER TEN

THE *quinta* was quiet and the night breathless with expectation. Kurt drew Rosalind into his arms and they kissed once more. Fire licked along her veins, her body responding willingly to his. When he released her lips at last, he brushed her cheek lightly with his thumb and murmured raggedly, 'I knew I still wanted you the second I saw you again. Each time we've been together since, I've wanted to make love to you.'

His breath was warm against her temple. She felt his lips graze her skin. Even before she allowed him to take her into the fold of his arm and lead her upstairs, her pulse was racing.

Inside his room he swept her off her feet and strode with her to the bed. He laid her on the covers, kissed her with tender hunger and while he did so lowered himself against her body.

She ran her fingers through his hair, need for him a fever in her blood.

'I love you,' she whispered.

'Tell me again,' he demanded.

Ripples of pleasure danced over her skin as he slipped the silk blouse from her shoulders. She felt him unfasten her bra.

'I love you,' she admitted helplessly, wanting him never to stop caressing the softness of her breasts and kissing her.

'God, you're so beautiful,' he breathed, his voice husky with passion.

Drawing away from her a little, he pulled off his shirt, tossing it aside before bending to claim her mouth once more. His kiss was a deep, needful invasion that made her feel hot and cold and shaky.

Her naked breasts were crushed softly against the warm hardness of his chest, the tangle of hair that matted it teasing her aroused nipples. The erotic sensations that pierced her were so sweet that she dug her fingers into his strong shoulders.

She sensed his dark, glittering gaze sweeping over her. He cupped her breast in his hand, his firm lips closing over her nipple, as he drew it into the warmth of his mouth. His tongue traced a circle around it before brushing the hard peak until she moaned with pleasure.

He rolled over on to his back, pulling her with him. As she pressed her lips to the strong column of his throat he whispered raggedly, 'Touch me.'

Weak and trembling, she obeyed him, her sensitive fingers, made bold by her need, caressing his hot skin. His muscles were lean and hard under the tangle of hair that narrowed to taper in a line down his strong torso. The iron feel of him thrilled her. Unable to see, she could yet conjure up in her mind the gleaming strength of his man's frame in her mind. Her fingers found the buckle of his belt and then timidly drew back.

With a low growl Kurt slid his palms down the whole length of her, making her wholly aware of his arousal. He shifted, his hands deftly removing her lace briefs as he pressed her back so that once again she lay beneath him.

It was the start of an inescapable and tantalisingly slow journey into a maze of desire. Stroking, licking, kissing, Kurt adored her, his hands expressing his delight in her body. She had never known anything so powerful as his lovemaking. In his arms she was pure woman, the centre of his world, just as he was the centre of hers.

She heard his voice muttering husky endearments and then gave a gasp as he touched her intimately. She flinched with the shock of exquisite pleasure that went through her.

In that instant Kurt's mouth found hers. His fingers continued to stroke her, his caresses featherlight, then deeper. On fire for him, she cried out, the agony of delight almost more than she could bear.

She had surrendered control to him almost completely, wanting him so desperately she gasped at last, scarcely knowing what she was saying, 'Now, Kurt. Please, now.'

He entered her then, the force of his desire tempered only by his care not to hurt her. She clutched at his shoulders, the pain of his first penetration forgotten almost instantly in the gathering storm of all-consuming pleasure.

Kurt withdrew on hearing her sob and then, as she arched towards him, he re-entered her, thrusting this time the full passionate way. Cleaving to him, she felt the ecstasy building up, the pitch of it becoming so intense that she sank her teeth into his shoulder, and then suddenly she was at the summit. The entire world seemed to explode in a burst of stars and light as her body began to shower her with pleasure.

She was falling, falling dizzily into freedom. Then she heard Kurt groan and a moment later her body was responding to him yet again, embracing him helplessly over and over before he shuddered against her.

Afterwards she lay dazed and throbbing with the force of what she had just experienced with him. As the hammer strokes of Kurt's heart slowed he drew her into his arms, cherishing her in the deep, satisfied afterglow that was so profound it seemed it would last forever.

The hand that stroked her back conveyed a message of tenderness and love. Her cheek against his chest, she felt him draw a long breath and then expel it in a sigh, more eloquent than words. His voice a tender, husky whisper he said softly, 'Sweetheart, you were wonderful.'

'I never dreamed it would be so beautiful,' she murmured before confessing, 'I always wanted to go to bed with you.'

'I thought you didn't believe in sex before marriage,' he said, teasing her gently.

A ghost of a laugh escaped her.

'It's a little late to remind me of that now...'

'Now that you're mine?' He guessed the rest of her sentence.

'I was always yours,' she whispered.

'Just as you always will be.'

She felt his lips brush her hair and then, the sweet tender ache inside her recalling the joy of oneness with him, she was slipping into a sleep that was as profound as the deep intimacy of their bodies.

When she awoke it was to feel the warm plane of Kurt's chest at her back and the weight of his arm across her naked waist. His breathing, which was steady and even, told her he was still asleep. Her lips curved into a drowsy smile as she lay for an instant luxuriating in the closeness of his strong body.

And then suddenly reality came back, filling her with a cold sense of inadequacy. The night of the fiesta was over. Now it was dawn and there was no avoiding thoughts of the future, thoughts which the previous evening, loving him, needing him, she had refused to pay heed to.

She wanted so much to share her life with him. Tears burned her eyes as she realised how impossible that was with things the way they were. As one overspilled and ran down her cheek she eased herself out of Kurt's slumberous embrace. Carefully, so as not to wake him, she slid off the bed and gathered up her clothes.

In her room she sank down in the chair near the window. She could feel the sun's warmth on her arms while the birds were beginning to sing sweetly in the all-pervading tranquillity. There was a tightness in her chest and her throat ached.

She had tried hard to come to terms with the blow fate had dealt her, and it was a long while since she had felt so desolate. Before, when regrets for the past had threatened to overwhelm her, she had escaped from them by losing herself in her work. But that charm had now lost the potency it had once had.

What am I going to do? she thought hopelessly. I love Kurt too much to deprive him of children. Tell him what the risks are, urged an inner voice. He may understand how you feel. It may make no difference.

But she did not believe the voice, and even if Kurt were to understand she couldn't bear to disappoint him, fail him. How could she ever be happy when all the time she would be haunted by the ghost of the family he might have had with someone else?

You'll have to tell him sooner or later, said the voice. But not now. Now now, when the memories of last night and of the next few days were going to have to last her for the rest of her life.

'Carpe diem', 'seize the day', her heart whispered. What harm could there be in making the most of every moment that was shot through with the magic of togetherness? She had known deep down at the fiesta that it couldn't last. She mustn't think of the future. For her the present must be enough.

She looked attractive and cool when, as the sun rose higher in the sky, she went downstairs and out on to the veranda. She slid her hands into the side-seam pockets of her trousers, drinking in the peaceful atmosphere. A faint prickling stirred at the back of her neck and she murmured questioningly, 'Kurt?'

'You're amazing,' came the chuckling reply. 'How do you do it?'

'Instinct, together with the fragrance of your aftershave,' she smiled, before asking, 'How long had you been standing there before I spoke?'

'Long enough to think how beautiful you are and how much I love you,' he said softly.

Her heart contracted with a bitter-sweet pain.

'Oh, Kurt...' she whispered.

'Come here,' he growled tenderly.

Unerringly she crossed the space that separated them. Kurt's arms went round her. She linked her hands behind his neck, meeting his tender-ardent kiss warmly and lovingly as he bent his head.

'What time did you slip away from me?' he asked. 'I missed you when I woke up this morning and you'd gone from my bed.'

'It was early, soon after dawn,' she said, the memories of their passionate lovemaking bringing a blush into her face.

His thumb stroked her cheek.

'Why didn't you stay?' he asked her, his voice devastatingly sensual.

'I... I couldn't.'

'Why not?'

'Julia... Julia might have seen me leaving your room.'

'And that would have embarrassed you.'

'A bit,' she said, attempting a smile.

'Pity,' he murmured huskily, his hands sliding beneath her top to feel the bareness of her warm back, 'or I could have enjoyed you all over again.'

The delicious tingle that traced down her spine put her sadness to flight. As they kissed she could think only of the thrill and excitement of loving him, even though it couldn't last.

'As an alternative to a cold shower, how about a swim before breakfast?' Kurt suggested in a throaty growl when reluctantly he released her lips. 'Go on, get your things.'

She went back upstairs and changed into her swimsuit. When she returned to the veranda Kurt was waiting for her.

'Very nice,' he commented approvingly.

A tingle of becoming colour came into her face. After last night it was ridiculous to feel shy with him, but the sensual note in his voice made her tantalisingly aware of the daring cut of her white swimsuit.

Kurt didn't take her arm, but, with his stride shortened companionably to match hers, walked beside her as they headed for the pool. Not till she felt the tiles cool beneath her bare feet did a capable hand guide her to the steps.

There was a muted splash as Kurt slid into the pool. She guessed he was standing by the steps, the water lapping his bronzed chest, as he waited to make sure she could find the rail without his help. Her assumption was proved correct as the moment her hand encountered it she felt the water surge, informing her that he was making towards the deep end in a powerful, effortless crawl.

Swimming parallel with the side of the pool, she followed him. Her breast-stroke was leisurely and graceful and as she approached the rail her hand reached out unerringly to grasp it.

'Don't tell me,' he said, a smile in his voice. 'You count each stroke.'

'Right,' she laughed, adding jokingly, 'I hope you're impressed.'

'I'm incredibly impressed.'

'I'm impressed too. With you,' she said, smiling back at him. 'You never treat me as if I'm different in any way, and yet I always know I'm safe with you.'

'I'd make good husband material,' he said.

Her heart gave a painful little lurch. A moment ago their banter had been light and easy. Now, although it sounded just the same, she knew instinctively that their conversation was getting serious. In an attempt not to let it, she said, 'For the right woman.'

She'd intended her remark to sound teasing but no quip came back in return. Unable to see his face, she didn't know what to make of his lack of reaction. Then he said quietly, 'What sort of answer is that?'

Averting her face so that he couldn't see her expression, she said in a desperate attempt to stop the exchange from going any further, 'I... I don't know what the question is.'

A hand turned her chin back towards him.

'I'm asking you to marry me,' Kurt said.

The anguish she felt was like a tight knot inside her. It took her an instant before she could steel herself to speak.

'I... I can't,' she said tonelessly, 'I shan't ever marry.'

Without waiting for his reply, she pushed off against the tiles, cleaving through the water in a crawl. She was cold with the misery of what she couldn't bring herself to tell him. All she wanted was to escape from him, to go back to the house, to flee from a conversation she couldn't handle.

As she neared the rail she changed to a breaststroke, her tears as she raised her head mingling with the droplets of water on her lashes. She groped for the steps and then gave a gasp as a strong hand encircled her wrist and hauled her bodily from the pool.

'Let go of me!' she demanded, her pent-up despair turning to unreasonable defiance.

'I want to know why you won't marry me.' Kurt's voice was calm and even.

She visualised him standing before her, his hair dark and sleek with moisture. Slicked off his face, it would emphasise the determined line of his jaw. She swallowed hard as she fought for composure.

'I've told you, I can't,' she repeated.

'Because you're blind?' he said. 'Is that why?'

The gentle note in his voice made her want to break down and cry. She was beginning to tremble and willed herself to control it.

'You can't tell me it makes no difference,' she said.

'Just what do I have to do to convince you?' Kurt demanded with curbed forcefulness. 'Surely you know by now that the fact that you're blind doesn't matter to me.'

'I...I know that's what you think,' she said. The tightness in her chest meant that even to draw breath was painful. 'But some day it would matter. Five years hence, ten years hence maybe. I don't know how long it would take, but you'd start to have regrets.'

'What makes you so sure of that?'

'Because I'd have regrets too.'

There was a pause. Then Kurt said, 'Then what exactly are you suggesting we do about our relationship?'

She bit her lip, gathering all her reserves of inner strength before answering, 'We...we end it the day you fly back to London.'

'Is that all this is to you—a holiday romance?' he said, taking hold of her impatiently by the shoulders.

'Yes! No...!' Now was the time to tell him, but she couldn't. How could she face up to his reaction when she couldn't cope with her own feelings of despair and disappointment? 'It can't be any more than a holiday romance!'

'Why the hell not?'

'Because... because my work's here and I'm not prepared to leave the island.' In her panic she was saying anything. She didn't care if she sounded hard. It was better to sound hard than to have to admit the truth, risk his rejection. 'I'm sorry, Kurt, but I like the life I have here on Madeira too much to give it up.'

'I can't believe I'm hearing you say this!' he said with muted ferocity. 'Last night you told me you loved me, told me not just with words but with that very expressive body of yours. Now this morning you're saying your work comes first!'

'It does come first! It has to come first!'

'I'm not asking you to give your work up,' he shot back. He drew a short breath, mastering his frustration with her before continuing, 'I know that your work's important to you, but I also know that you believe in commitment and that nothing short of marriage would be enough for either of us. Look, you can have any kind of studio you want. Just tell me the layout you need and I'll design it for you.'

'You don't understand,' she whispered wretchedly.

'Well, damn it, I'm trying to. Are you afraid that marriage might somehow sap your creative talent or is it that if we had a family...'

'I don't want a family,' she cut across him. Her voice was unsteady and it took all her courage to continue, 'I like my life as it is. It's rewarding enough for me. I don't need marriage and children to feel fulfilled. I'll... I'll come to London with you if you want me to. I'll live with you there, but I won't marry you.'

'I see.' His tone was expressionless. 'And for how long will you stay with me?'

'I don't know,' she said jerkily. 'If you want a family...'

As her voice caught he cut in roughly, 'So you're saying that all you want is a short-term affair?'

'I'm sorry,' she cried. 'I'm sorry, but yes, that's all we can ever have!'

'Well, thanks a lot.'

She flinched at his cold sarcasm that deliberately flayed her.

'Why couldn't you have left things as they were?' she hissed almost in tears.

Knowing she had to get away before she broke down completely, she turned, hurrying back towards the house. Her blindness slowed her flight and she was sobbing by the time she reached the veranda. Kurt didn't follow her.

CHAPTER ELEVEN

DRAINED of tears but not of grief, Rosalind sought refuge later that morning in her studio. She plunged her fists deep in the pockets of her smock. She wanted to think clearly but, each time she tried, emotion gained the upper hand, making it impossible.

She could no more put everything that had happened into any kind of perspective than she could work out what she was going to say to Kurt the next time they were alone together. She only knew that it was inevitable that there would be a sequel to their confrontation. Kurt was serious about her, and he wasn't a man to give up, no matter what barriers she tried to erect between them.

A tap at the door startled her. Hurriedly she brushed her hand across her damp cheeks and drew the damaged sculpture of mother and child towards her so that it would look as if she was working.

She guessed it was Julia, and she didn't want her aunt to know she had been crying. Julia would ask what was wrong, and at the moment she couldn't talk about it. She was too numb, too desolate.

It took a fierce effort of will to sound composed and in charge of herself as she called out, 'Come in.'

She heard the door open.

'I thought this would be where I'd find you.'

She pivoted in alarm, her heart thumping as she recognised Kurt's voice.

'What... what do you want?' she breathed.

'I'm driving to Camacha to have another look at the building plot. I wondered if you'd like to come. We can stop off for coffee somewhere.'

His tone was pleasant and casual, as if their exchange by the pool had never taken place. It confused her, as did the gathering in the air, the sense of kismet. She turned back to the work bench. Her hands were trembling and she clenched them tightly. She wasn't ready for a second confrontation so soon after the first.

Swallowing hard, she said, 'Thanks, but I... I'd rather stay here.'

'And I'd rather you came with me.'

His voice held an unmistakable ring of authority and, pushed on to the defensive, she reacted with a quick flare of anger. He had no right to force her into conflict with her feelings like this.

'Can't you see it's no use?' she flashed as she swung back to face him.

'What's no use?'

'Us! This! Everything!' The words were torn from her.

Kurt didn't reply at once. She sensed his blue gaze on her, but, unable to see, she had no idea what to make of his silence. She only knew that he stood before her, tall, forceful and invincible.

His stillness made her think that some kind of attack was imminent and she braced herself inwardly for it. As two capable hands descended on her shoulders she caught her breath imperceptibly. But to her surprise his grip conveyed no message of angry ferocity. Instead, like his voice, it was unexpectedly gentle.

'You're not the sort of woman to give yourself lightly,' he stated quietly. 'If you didn't believe in our relationship you wouldn't have slept with me last night. Just as you wouldn't be saying now that you'll live with me.'

Almost afraid to hope, she faltered, 'Is... is that what you want? For me to live with you?'

'If you remember, you said that was all you could offer me,' he answered.

He was neither crowding her nor bludgeoning her, and as he drew her close she offered no resistance. She ran her fingers along the lapel of his jacket, her unseeing gaze level with the second button of his shirt.

'It is,' she confirmed in a whisper.

'Then, as I've decided living together is better than nothing, why don't we kiss and make up?'

She raised her head, her heart lurching. She couldn't believe that he was accepting her terms, that there was a chance for them to be happy together even though their relationship must ultimately end. But for now that chance was enough, more than enough. A catch in her voice, she said, smiling tremulously, 'I'd... I'd like that more than anything.'

Taking her face in his hands, he bent his head. It was a long, lingering kiss, passionate yet tender, and she knew without any doubt he was telling her that, married or not, they belonged together, that she was his woman. And when finally his lips left hers he confirmed it with words.

Holding her close, he said against her cheek, 'I love you, sweetheart.'

'I love you, too,' she confessed willingly.

'Enough to tear yourself away from your studio until lunchtime?' he asked with gentle humour. 'We ought to be back from Camacha by then.'

Suddenly she was laughing, happier than she had any right to be.

'Enough to go anywhere with you,' she told him.

In the car Kurt kept up an easy conversation with her. It had all come right, she thought marvelling. Yet for how long would he find it enough living with a woman who appeared not to share his desire for a family? she wondered uneasily. She pushed the thought away. She was going to let no shadow fall across the present by looking into the future.

'How soon do you want me to join you in London?' she asked.

'What's wrong with our flying back together at the end of the week?' he said.

'You're not giving me much time!' she laughed.

'I'm not risking your changing your mind,' he said with humour, his hand leaving the wheel briefly to squeeze hers.

'We'll have to tell Julia,' she murmured, a faint furrow appearing between her brows.

'What's the problem?' Kurt asked. 'She knows you and I are in love with each other. I don't think our decision's going to come as any great surprise to her.'

But it was going to surprise her father. Rosalind wasn't at all sure how he was going to react when she informed him that she intended living with her ex-fiancé in London. She was very fond of him and she respected his opinions, but, she reasoned, she was an adult, free to make her own choices. Somehow she would make him understand that she wanted to live with Kurt and not to marry him.

'There isn't a problem,' she said. 'I... I was just thinking aloud.'

'I was afraid you were having second thoughts already,' he quipped.

'Of course I'm not.' She smiled.

As the car drew to a halt she asked, 'Are we there already?'

'Yes, we're at the building plot.' He got out of the Mercedes to open her door for her. 'When the house is finished Julia's going to have the most incredible views,' he commented.

His voice told her he was gazing at the mountains, his eyes crinkling in the bright light.

'It will be even lovelier than at the *quinta*,' she agreed, picturing the setting in her mind, the lush valley that lay below them and the steep slopes that were clad in pine groves and mimosa.

Faintly she could hear the sound of distant waterfalls singing. All else was stillness. The sunshine was hot on her skin and in the perfect contentment of the moment there seemed no need for words. At one with their surroundings, they strolled to the low white wall that marked the far boundary of the property.

She touched the roughness of the sun-warmed stone.

'Well, I think this is as good a place as any,' Kurt announced.

'You mean for the house?' she queried, and then teased, 'That sounds a bit slap-happy for an eminent architect.'

'I wasn't thinking about the house,' he informed her. 'I meant this is as good a place as any for you to tell me why you won't marry me.'

For an instant shock robbed her of her voice. The colour drained from her face and she knew that her emotion must be visible.

She should have realised he'd agreed to her terms far too easily. He'd appeared to go along with her when all the time he must have been planning this manoeuvre. He'd asked her to come here with him deliberately, knowing they couldn't be interrupted and that she couldn't bolt to the safety of her studio.

'You said...you agreed we were going to live together!' she began, her voice unsteady, 'You had no right to bring me here under false pretenses, to——'

'What false pretences?' he interrupted impatiently, 'I love you, Rosalind. In what way is that a pretence? I want to marry you, and there's nothing false about that, either.'

Angrily she accused, 'You let me think——'

'That I was never going to mention the topic of marriage again?' he cut in. Quietly but forcefully he went on, 'Well, come up with one good reason why you won't marry me and maybe I'll agree to let the subject drop.'

She perched on the wall as though her legs suddenly would support her no longer. She recognised that quietly determined edge to his voice that insisted upon an answer.

She tried to gather her strength. She wanted to share her pain with him but she was so afraid. It wasn't a fear she could rationalise. She knew him better now than to think, as she had done once, that he was going to reject her simply because she couldn't give him a son.

You have to tell him, insisted a voice she had refused to heed when it had spoken before. She swallowed against the constriction in her voice.

'All right,' she began huskily. 'I . . . I'm not good enough for you.'

It was as far as she got.

'So that is the reason,' Kurt cut in in an angry undertone.

'Kurt, please, please will you listen?' she sobbed.

'No, you're going to listen,' he told her, pulling her to her feet so roughly that she gave a little gasp. 'Suppose I'd been the one who'd lost my sight, would it have altered your feelings for me?' he demanded.

'I . . . No, but that's not the point!' she cried.

'Damn it, woman, it is the point,' he contradicted with fierce emphasis. 'I loved you before I knew you were suffering from a hereditary eye disease. I love you now. It makes no difference to me that you're blind. How many times do I have to tell you before you'll believe me? Do I have to go down on my knees to convince you?'

Her fingers tightened on his arms. He had used the word 'hereditary'. He knew! She felt as if he had snatched her out of some dark pit and even though she was blind it was like being dazzled by brilliance.

'What... what did you say?' she breathed. 'Who... who told you?'

'Who told me what?' he asked.

'That if we have children they may inherit my blindness.'

'You mean... You mean that's what this has all been about?' Kurt said, suddenly understanding.

'I didn't know how to tell you,' she whispered shakily, unable all at once to take in the miracle of his love. 'I thought...'

As her voice caught, Kurt hugged her close. She clung to him, trembling and in tears, crying not with despair as she had once but with relief that he still wanted her. Kurt held her tightly, his hand smoothing her hair.

'That's why you said you'd live with me and wouldn't marry me.'

'Yes,' she gulped.

Easing her away from him a little, he brushed away her tears with two gentle thumbs.

'There's equally a chance that if we have children they won't inherit your blindness,' he told her.

'I'm not a gambler, Kurt,' she whispered. 'I've thought and thought about it, and I simply can't take the risk.'

'Your parents did.'

'My mother didn't know a rare eye disease ran in her family.'

'And if she had, would you have blamed her for your blindness?'

'No... I... of course not. How could I blame her for giving me life?' she said.

Suddenly she was seeing the situation in a whole new light. It was as though Kurt had handed her back her dreams, everything she had ever wanted. But did she have the courage to take what he offered? As if reading her mind, he said gently, 'I'm not saying there isn't a problem, that deciding to have children isn't going to be a big step, something we're going to have to think about together. All I'm saying is together we can make the decision that's right for us.'

'Oh, Kurt...' she said huskily. 'All this time you've understood and I didn't know. Was it Julia who told you?'

'Not about the hereditary factor, or rather not in so many words. When I asked after you, she said you'd lost your sight through Leber's disease. I'd never heard of it. I contacted a friend of mind who's an eye specialist. I had to find out more, not least to understand what it must be like for you. I hadn't forgiven you. I was furious with you over Andrew, yet what made me even angrier was the thought that he must have split up with you because of your blindness. That was when I realised I was still in love with you, and that didn't improve my temper either.'

The wry note in his voice made her smile. She put her arms up round his neck, feeling almost drunk with the wonder of it all.

'You didn't act as if you were still in love with me,' she chided.

'Come to that, neither did you,' he laughed. Bending his head, he grazed her lips with his, before murmuring, 'Don't ever let me hear you say again that you're not good enough for me or that you need to see the look in my eyes to believe me.' His arms tightened around her. 'You're my first love, my only love, for always.'

And, kissing him back with a response that was as fierce as his demand, she believed him.

Next month's Romances

Each month, you can choose from a world of variety in romance with Mills & Boon. These are the new titles to look out for next month.

DANGEROUS INTERLOPER Penny Jordan
BETRAYED Anne Mather
TEMPT ME NOT Susan Napier
FORBIDDEN ENCHANTMENT Patricia Wilson
STAY UNTIL DAWN Elizabeth Oldfield
LASTING LEGACY Kay Thorpe
FORBIDDEN PASSION Sarah Holland
OUTBACK MAN Miranda Lee
MAN OF TRUTH Jessica Marchant
CARIBBEAN DESIRE Cathy Williams
SHADOW IN THE WINGS Lee Stafford
RISK OF THE HEART Grace Green
THE PARIS TYPE Christine Greig
HEARTSONG Melinda Cross
THE OTHER WOMAN Jessica Steele

STARSIGN
FORTUNE IN THE STARS Kate Proctor

Available from Boots, Martins, John Menzies, W.H. Smith, Woolworths and other paperback stockists.

Also available from Mills and Boon Reader Service, P.O. Box 236, Thornton Road, Croydon, Surrey CR9 3RU.

COMING IN SEPTEMBER

The eagerly awaited new novel from this internationally bestselling author. Lying critically injured in hospital, Liz Danvers implores her estranged daughter to return home and read her diaries. As Sage reads she learns of painful secrets in her mothers hidden past, and begins to feel compassion and a reluctant admiration for this woman who had stood so strongly between herself and the man she once loved. The diaries held the clues to a number of emotional puzzles, but the biggest mystery of all was why Liz had chosen to reveal her most secret life to the one person who had every reason to resent and despise her.

Available: September 1991. Price £4.99

W●RLDWIDE

From: Boots, Martins, John Menzies, W.H. Smith,
Woolworths and other paperback stockists.
Also available from Reader Service, Thornton Road,
Croydon Surrey, CR9 3RU

While away the lazy days of late Summer with our new gift selection
Intimate Moments

Four Romances, new in paperback, from four favourite authors.
The perfect treat!

The Colour of the Sea
Rosemary Hammond

Had We Never Loved
Jeneth Murrey

The Heron Quest
Charlotte Lamb

Magic of the Baobab
Yvonne Whittal

Available from July 1991. Price: £6.40

Available from Boots, Martins, John Menzies, W.H. Smith, Woolworths and other paperback stockists.
Also available from Mills and Boon Reader Service,
P.O. Box 236, Thornton Road, Croydon, Surrey CR9 3RU.

Do you long to escape to romantic, exotic places?

To a different world – a world of romance?

THE PAGES OF A MILLS & BOON WILL TAKE YOU THERE

Look out for the special Romances with the FARAWAY PLACES stamp on the front cover, and you're guaranteed to escape to distant shores, to share the lives and loves of heroes and heroines set against backgrounds of faraway, exotic locations.

There will be one of these special Romances every month for 12 months. The first is set on the beautiful island of Tobago in the Caribbean.

Available from September, 1991 at:

Boots, Martins, John Menzies, W.H. Smith, Woolworths and other paperback stockists.

Also available from Mills and Boon Reader Service, P.O. Box 236, Thornton Road, Croydon, Surrey CR9 3RU.

4 FREE
Romances
and 2 FREE gifts
just for you!

*You can enjoy all the
heartwarming emotion of true love for FREE!
Discover the heartbreak and the happiness, the emotion
and the tenderness of the modern relationships in
Mills & Boon Romances.*

We'll send you 4 captivating Romances as a special offer
from Mills & Boon Reader Service, along with the chance to
have 6 Romances delivered to your door each month.

Claim your FREE books and gifts overleaf...

An irresistible offer from Mills & Boon

Here's a personal invitation from Mills & Boon Reader Service, to become a regular reader of Romances. To welcome you, we'd like you to have 4 books, a CUDDLY TEDDY and a special MYSTERY GIFT absolutely FREE.

Then you could look forward each month to receiving 6 brand new Romances, delivered to your door, postage and packing free! Plus our free newsletter featuring author news, competitions, special offers and much more.

This invitation comes with no strings attached. You may cancel or suspend your subscription at any time, and still keep your free books and gifts.

It's so easy. Send no money now. Simply fill in the coupon below and post it to -
Reader Service, FREEPOST, PO Box 236, Croydon, Surrey CR9 9EL.

--- NO STAMP REQUIRED ---

Free Books Coupon

Yes! Please rush me my 4 free Romances and 2 free gifts! Please also reserve me a Reader Service subscription. If I decide to subscribe I can look forward to receiving 6 brand new Romances each month for just £9.60, postage and packing free. If I choose not to subscribe I shall write to you within 10 days - I can keep the books and gifts whatever I decide. I may cancel or suspend my subscription at any time. I am over 18 years of age.

Name Mrs/Miss/Ms/Mr _____ EP18R

Address _____

_____

Postcode _____ Signature _____

Offer expires 31st May 1992. The right is reserved to refuse an application and change the terms of this offer. Readers overseas and in Eire please send for details. Southern Africa write to Independant Book Services, Postbag X3010, Randburg 2125.
You may be mailed with offers from other reputable companies as a result of this application.
If you would prefer not to share in this opportunity, please tick box ☐